The arena mirrored lined the walls lik room was circular with wide cement seats, which were smooth and blended seamlessly together. The ring, known as the cage, sat at its center. A vaulted ceiling went so far up Tommy could not see the inner dome.

Human remains lay everywhere. The fighter watched the lingering crowd file out of the underground stadium as he paced the mat, letting the blood roll up over the tops of his feet.

Four men in blue jumpsuits entered the cage with mop buckets and scrub brushes. All four hesitated as the fighter eyed them carefully but said nothing. Finally, the men went about the task of cleaning the cage. When the fighter had had enough of playing in the gore, he left the cage without a word.

STRANGE ROADS

BY STEVEN LLOYD

MACABRE INK

For Ovid
He Knows why.

CONTENTS

INTRODUCTION

I owe Steven Lloyd a cup of coffee. I have for about a decade, ever since my first novel was released and he asked to do an interview for *Kingdom of Shadows*. He was my first and (though I'm not sure) I think I was also his, so thanks to the net we exchanged emails with questions and answers sailing back and forth. For those of you who have done these things, you know questions tend to be general: Why do you like writing horror? Who are your favorite writers? What frightens the Father of Nightmares?... What? Actually it was that last question that will forever standout much more than my answer, which I don't really remember. Still after doing a dozen interviews, that question will be the only one I remember.

Ten years passed and I get an email from Dave Dinsmore of Biting Dog Pubs asking me to read a story they planned on releasing, "The Wooden Box" by Steven. I did—I told him I loved it. Another year passes and I receive a message asking if I'd be willing to do the introduction for *Strange Roads* (with a copy of the stories). Rule 1 for such requests: Only put your name on work you like. Only once didn't I follow this. As a favor I praised a novella that I actually didn't like, because—well some of us scratch backs in the business. Needless to say such actions can easily destroy one's credibility so I stopped doing such things until now. I sat and read the seven stories you've got in your hands and said, "Wow."

Wow—I said it again this morning as I finished reading *Strange Roads* for the third time. If you're new to Steven Lloyd's work, you'll be saying it too as you read the following seven tales and a taste of an upcoming project. The collection begins with "The Wooden Box." If you've read it before I suggest you do it again, because it is a nice welcome for what follows. This tale of love and ultimate sacrifice guides its readers into the uniqueness of his work, the understanding that stories can stir the soul without being immersed in blood and gore.

There is no letup beyond "The Wooden Box" and I think you'll love the way he draws you in to characters who attempt to conquer whatever has been laid before them. We have a fighter battling the ultimate opponent, a man who battles for what is his—in spite of the consequences, a sin is uncovered and paid for, and two brothers with an evil secret. Beyond these, Steven shares his YA tale "Where There Be Dragons," which is a nice breather to close the collection.

Don't shut the book until you check out Steven's interview. I actually read this section before getting into the stories, because I find knowing the whys adds to the enjoyment of reading and he shares just enough to bring the reader closer to the work. Whether you do so before or after, once finished take a few minutes to reflect then do others a favor. Spread the word about Steven Lloyd and *Strange Roads*—not because he's a friend, relative or fellow writer, but because he's damn good and people love discovering good storytellers before they become household names, and this deserves to be shared.

That said, I was just looking over my notes and smiled because the question hit me in the face again: What frightens the Father of Nightmares? I'm not afraid of monsters—zombies, werewolves, vampires, whatever. They aren't real and they don't force me to lock my doors at night. It's stories like the ones in this collection that frighten me—tales seeded with the darker emotions of human nature. It is writers like Steven Lloyd who do it to me and I'm sure he'll make many of you feel the same way.

—John Paul Allen
Springfield, TN
September 2014

THE WOODEN BOX

Mack Grainy didn't notice the sun going down. He'd been working in the barn, chiseling away at the smooth pine box ever since Nora took ill six months ago. As he stood up to stretch his legs, he heard a flutter of wings.

About a year ago, an owl made its residence in the rafters. At night, if you took a mind to, you could stay up and watch it come and go from the barn to the meadow searching for rats. Most times, though, it just hooted a lot. Kind of raised the hair on the back of your neck if you've never heard one before.

The barn itself, a towering structure of aged cedar and oak consisted of a loft and four central stalls, all of which stood empty except the one on the end. That was Minny's. Minny was their last and only livestock, a kicking rough neck of a mule that'd plant your face to the other side if she didn't know you. Mack wanted to eliminate the stall gate at one time or another, but Minny kicked the damn thing off its rusting hinges one night. Guess she liked it that way. She'd go out and graze in the morning, trot back in the afternoon. They let her have the run of the barn.

Mack finished for the day, threw a tarp over the box, then went to the house.

Inside he sat at the kitchen table, rolled up a badly wrinkled newspaper. He swatted an assemblage of flies perched on the table. He missed all but three. "Damn things," he said. They scuttled up the walls and kitchen counters. He knew why they were here. Nora. They were waiting for her to die. He wanted things to be normal again, like they used to be. But that wasn't going to happen. He faced the facts a long time ago. She was dying and there was nothing to be done about it. He smacked the table again scattering the winged bandits into the air. No matter how much tape he hung from the ceiling, they kept coming.

Cancer stole Nora's leg this past winter. Toenails rotted away, and then her foot went all grayish-black. She'd lost it from the knee down. That was that. She lost her will right then and there. Due to the fact that the doctors hadn't overlapped enough tissue to smooth out the stump, the bone jutted out like an ivory-colored fence post that'd been gnawed on. The cancer spread so fast there was nothing else that could be done. They gave her six months to a year.

He left the table, filled a pot with water. He placed it on the cookstove to warm. Even in the summer, when the heat came on without mercy, and before the illness stole her, she loved a warm bath. He collected two rags, one for drying, the other for washing, placed them over one wide shoulder, and walked into the bedroom.

Nora was lying beneath four quilts. Her eyes were closed. By the time he'd placed the pot on the nightstand and sat down, she opened her eyes. "Thought you gone and forgot me," she said.

"Never," Mack said as he soaked a rag, lathered it up with soap. "Been busy is all."

"Cain't cook. Cain't even get outta bed no more," she said. "Done with my box?"

"Why you in such a hurry to die, Nora? I want you around for a bit."

She'd been a hell of a cook in her day. When they had the chili cook-off, four counties converged on the small town of Goreville. Nora won each year.

Then there were the four travelers last year. Said they came from East Texas. Mack'd seen his fair share of rag-tags, but these four had had it bad. They'd looked like they'd been chewed up and spit out. Life had done this. No mercy for those on the road. They'd asked about work. Mack told them no work needed done, so Nora invited them to bed down in the barn and a meal. She'd cooked up a mess of white beans, cornbread, and taters. The next morning they were gone. Mack had gone out to the barn to fetch them for breakfast, but they'd skipped out sometime before dawn. Mack tore away from the thoughts when he heard Nora.

"Macky," she said softly. "When's it gonna be time?"

Only two women called him that, and one of 'em been gone morin' thirty years. Man called him that he'd split their skull with a fist or axe handle. "Don't you worry none," Mack said. "You get your rest. I'll deal with all that." Looking around the room, he took in the wallpaper. Flowers. God, how she loved the damn things.

Once Nora called from the house for Mack to de-weed the flowers around the house. Though she loved her flowers, Nora hated de-weeding them. Whatever caused her to think he liked doing it was beyond him. Had it been his way, they'd never been planted.

An hour later he'd stepped into the house for a jar of water and to sit a spell. He noticed her sitting at the table and thought he'd best get on out to the barn. Make himself busy, case she wanted the house painted.

Mack was almost to the door when she asked, "You de-weed them plants?"

"Course," he'd said. "That's what I been doin' since you told me to. Why? Got something else for me to do?" He answered too quickly, God knows, and she got up, pushed the chair under the table. He had de-weeded them, not just in the way she would've liked. Truth to tell, he'd pulled up every last one of 'em. In that moment he'd wished those damn flowers would've sprouted back up in a hurry, 'cause Nora had gone all stiff like. Her eyes narrowed.

"Did, huh," she'd said, easing herself toward the door. "Do a good job?"

Mack put his hand on the brass doorknob, hoping to keep her inside a while longer. And when she'd reached the door he'd felt a single line of sweat drip off the end of his nose. "Good as I could, yes," Mack said. "What you doin'?" he asked, blocking the door a little more. "Too dang hot out there. I took care of it. No need goin' out there."

Her eyes'd gone all wild then, and she'd leapt on him like a rabid bobcat, hitting and slapping. Mack took the punches, and managed to open the door and stumble outside onto the porch. By then she'd crawled from his front to his back and was pounding something awful when she saw the yard brightly lit in different colors. He'd felt a few of them punches. Mack found her swinging arm and pulled hard, throwing her off of him and into the yard. She'd hit the ground so hard dust kicked up all around her. He got scared and ran to her. He picked her up and dusted her off, asked if she was all right. She was. A moment later they were in stitches and fixing to bust.

"Meanest man in four counties, huh," she'd said laughing. "Cain't wait till the girls in town hear this."

Mack was doubled over laughing. "Better not," he'd said between fits of laughter. But his laughter was short lived as Nora took to her feet, crossed her arms against her chest.

"You plant them flowers back this spring, Macky Grainy," Nora had said. "Or I'll spill the beans, and our bed will be a little less filled. You hear?"

So Mack agreed and replanted those infernal things the following spring. Plus Nora kept her promise, which he was grateful for.

Six months later the depression hit. Two years after that the cancer found Nora.

Now he was cleaning and washing bedsores. Some oozed greenish puss, while others were quarter sized and gaping. He poured peroxide in the deep ones. She screamed and swatted and cussed 'til the pain ebbed and she was out of breath. Mack never faulted her for it.

Finished, he placed the rags in the pot. He disappeared into the other room. He came back with her wheelchair. He put her in that, and then stripped the bedding. Mack collected fresh linen from a chest of drawers, made the bed. Then he laid her on the bed again and covered her. Mack was turning to leave when she asked the question she kept asking since the cancer took over.

"You gone do it soon, Macky?" she asked. "Can you still do it?"

Mack stood at the door with his back to her. He had nothing. Words escaped him. And then he finally said, "I can." Tears welled up in his eyes. "I can do it."

"When?"

"Soon," Mack said. "Soon."

"How soon, Macky?" she asked. "Cause the pains startin' to come more now. I can't live like this."

"I know," said Mack. His hands trembled so badly the pot of water threatened to slip from his grasp. He turned to face her. "A few days. All right? I promise."

Nora said nothing more and closed her eyes. Soon he heard the rhythm of her breathing and left the room. He put the pot in the sink. He found the good book in an old china cabinet. Its cover was black leather and tattered, the pages torn from handling and age. The words Holy Bible had virtually faded away. Mack ran his strong, liver-spotted hand along its aged exterior. Nora had read the book cover to cover over the years to the point the bindings had split and frayed.

He should've bought her a new one. Mack had never been the religious type. All the things he'd done in his youth and later in the war, he expected his hands to catch fire when he touched its cover, but they didn't. He opened the book, fumbled clumsily through the blasted thing until he found the verse she wanted inscribed on the box. He read the verse for the first time and cried.

The next morning Nora and Mack ate breakfast in silence. Their eyes met a few times, but no words were exchanged. After they finished Mack was collecting their plates, when Nora touched his wrist and stared up into his dark brown eyes.

"Today?" asked Nora. "Is it today?"

"Not today," Mack said. "Got the inscription to finish. But soon."

"Wish we could dance like we once did," Nora said. "Sure could use some of that. 'member?"

"I do," Mack said swallowing back tears. "You could really kick up them heels."

On Friday nights Mack and Nora used to turn on the music

box and tear up the living room dancing. They drank from the jug, and before the night ended they were tripping over one another, tangled together so badly a pry bar could not have peeled them apart. They made funny in bed until the sun bled through the trees. When they'd finally pulled themselves out of bed in the afternoon, their heads pounded and bones ached.

Mack left the room and cleaned the plates. When he looked in on her again he saw she'd fallen asleep. This might not be as bad as the doctors warned, Mack thought. Might be all she'd get. He could deal with this, even though she was still asking him to do it. Perhaps she'd just slip away peacefully in her sleep.

He was wrong.

The next week Nora's pain burrowed in deep as if it had claws and a mind of its own, made its home in her bones. Her flesh took on a yellowish-green hue. She was near skeletal now at eighty-five pounds. Her once vibrant eyes were sunk back within their sockets, and her movements were limited.

Mack split his day between the barn and caring for Nora. He sat down next to the wooden box, pulled on a jug of lightening old man Peters dropped off few days ago. Old man Peters was their local postman. They shared many a drink together over the years.

Then he went back to work, cutting out the words Nora wanted, all under the watchful eye of Minny. Once she sauntered over and nudged him with her head, something she never did. Mack expected to get a mouth full of horseshoe, but that didn't happen.

After a while his hands got to hurting so he got up and swept out Minny's stall and filled her water. He brought her in some fresh hay. It gave him time to think of something other than that damn old box, which to be honest, he was proud of. He knew Nora would love it and that's all that mattered.

Finished with Minny, Mack swept out the entire barn. At the work bench, he gathered up what tools he wasn't using, put them away. They were scattered to hell and back. It needed to be done. Mack came upon his old trench mace. A short wooden handled club with a steel ball and jutting spikes on the business end. He'd used it a few times after taking it from a German officer in a trench. Made a real mess of a fella if you used it right. A few Germans lost their jaws, teeth and gums under its weight.

And without warning it hit him full in the chest, his body, his mind, and his soul. It bathed over him so strongly he couldn't keep it down any longer. Mack Grainy cried long and hard.

Minny snorted, tapped the earthen floor playfully as if she understood. She walked over to Mack and nudged him again.

It was time.

Mack found Nora awake. The screaming passed an hour ago. The doctors gave them morphine for when the pain settled in. It came in real handy. She was alert, as if she knew by the look on his face. But before she could ask, Mack said, "In the morning. No sooner. I want us to watch the sunrise together," he said as he watched her face beam. It was almost as if she were young again. That vibrant, colorful girl he'd met just after the war. She'd hate him for leaving the farm once she was gone, but he felt it better not to tell her. No need making her last few hours heart-wrenching. No need stayin' around here without her. It'd just bring back long, lost memories he wouldn't be able to bear.

Mack sat next to her on the bed for a long time. He held her frail, cold hand for the last time.

In the morning before dawn, Mack wheeled in the chair, woke her. Her eyes fluttered open, confused for a moment and then remembered. "Ready?" Mack asked.

"Been ready," she said. "You?"

"No," Mack said. "Rather Minny kick me in the teeth than do this."

"It'll be over soon."

Mack said, "Want you to see the box first. Figure it took me six months to build it, least you could do is see it."

In the barn, Nora ran her hands along the smooth wooden box. The varnish gleamed under the oil lamp's amber light. It hung by a nail in a beam next to the box. "Guess this is where all the coffee went, huh?"

"Makes for good varnish," Mack said. "Besides, you quit drinking coffee years ago." He ran his hand through her thinning gray hair. It was long, flowing and soft. She'd made sure to have him wash it every day. It was the only thing on her that didn't carry the scent of death.

"Pick me up," she said. "I want to read the inscription." He did. She ran her hands along the verse. She read it aloud as if it were her final attempt to save his soul. Mack didn't have the heart to stop her.

"The Lord is my Shepherd; I shall not want. He maketh me to lie down in green pastures: He leadeth me beside the still waters." She stopped and looked back at him. "We have time?"

"We got time," Mack said. "You been goin' through the shadow of death all these months. You've earned the right to finish it."

"He restoreth my soul: He leadeth me in the paths of righteousness for His name's sake. Yea, though I walk through the valley of the shadow of death, I will fear no evil: For thou art with me; Thy rod and thy staff, they comfort me. Thou preparest a table before me in the presence of mine enemies; Thou annointest my head with oil; My cup runneth over. Surely goodness and mercy shall follow me all the days of my life, and I will dwell in the House of the Lord forever." She looked up into those big brown eyes of his. Held onto him the best she could. "You done real good, Macky. So good." She saw Minny then. A make-shift trailer was hitched to her. The trailer was at an angle low enough to slide the box up onto. Minny stared back at her. She didn't move. She almost looked frightening in the light's amber glow. "Now," Nora said, "let's get to that sunrise."

Mack wheeled her to the back of the house for the event. He thought about things as they went. He thought about the farm and what would happen to it once he was gone. Surprisingly enough, he wondered if Nora's God would greet him as a friend when it was his time or would Nora be there to greet him at a place she said was the pearly gates. If all that was true, would he walk with her on streets of gold?

They were at the back of the house when the light seeped through the trees. The early dawn sky turned a bloodshot red, and soon the sky shifted in brighter colors.

Mack stood next to his wife of fifty years, hand on her shoulder. They did not speak. No pain could've been bad enough to tear this moment away from them. For now she was at peace. For now the pain could not touch her. When the sun was even with the tree tops, Mack leaned down, kissed her cheek gently and stepped back.

He fished his revolver out of his pocket and put one round in the back of her head. The impact nearly sent her out of the wheelchair.

Mack stood there long after the sun had risen. He cried so hard he thought he might have broken some ribs, or at least fractured some. Long after the cool morning air turned hot and sticky and breathtaking, Mack wheeled her to the barn, laid her in the box and nailed the lid down, all under the watchful eye of Minny. He tapped Minny's ass gently, guiding her out back of the barn.

A few months ago he dug up a place for Nora with the tractor. Mack backed Minny up toward the hole and when she was where he needed her, he slid the box off the trailer. He unhitched Minny, leaving her without the burden of the trailer. She ambled back to the barn.

Mack sat next to the box, and as Nora had done, he ran his hand along the box. "You're at peace now, ole girl," he said. There wasn't much left to do. His breath caught in his throat as he put the revolver under his chin and pulled the trigger.

A week later, Brian Peters found the hole, the box and Mack when he delivered the post. Not soon after that, he discovered Minny gave up the ghost, too. She lay on the stall floor stiff as a board. Flies got to her pretty bad. The whole barn smelt of her. Guess she figured with the two gone, she had nothing left to give.

Brian drove back into town forgetting about delivering the mail for the day, and got help. They finished what Mack started. They buried all three bodies properly.

Three weeks later, Brian Peters was driving past the old Grainy farm and saw something that caused his chest to hitch. A single light burned in the farm's window, and inside he saw two people kicking up their heels dancing as if they were having the time of their lives.

THE FIGHT OF THE CENTURY

Human remains lay everywhere. The fighter watched the lingering crowd file out of the underground stadium as he paced the mat, letting the blood roll up over the tops of his feet.

Four men in blue jumpsuits entered the cage with mop buckets and scrub brushes. All four hesitated. The fighter eyed them carefully, but said nothing. Finally the men began the task of cleaning the cage. When the fighter had had enough of playing in the gore, he left the cage without a word.

Chick's Bar was surprisingly calm for a Friday night.

Tommy Morrison sat at the bar. His head swam. He finished his fifth shot of whiskey and felt that familiar haze coming on. Cigarette smoke hung in the room. Got to quit this life, he thought. He stretched his arms and signaled the bartender. "One more for the road, Dale?" That's when the cue stick connected solidly against his ribs. Tommy toppled off the bar stool, shot glass flying.

Jimmy Coulter, Ralph Randal, and Pete Malcolm stood over him.

"Got the money, Tommy?" asked Jimmy.

When Tommy got his breath, he looked up at the big man, and said, "Nope. Couldn't come alone to ask?"

"Guy's crazy," Ralph said.

"Grab his feet, boys," Jimmy said. "We'll take him out back and talk." With that they dragged him away from the bar mantel. Tommy got one leg free and gave a good kick that connected with Pete's nose, which snapped. The bridge of his nose split open a half inch and blood poured out all over, soaking his face and shirt in seconds.

Pete howled as he fell backwards, arms flapping as he tried to grab something to stop his fall. He did not find anything, and toppled over a table.

Before they dragged him out the back door, Tommy thought he saw a man sitting in the back of the bar in a booth watching. The man seemed amused.

Tommy lay on the alley floor. Rainwater seeped through the back of his jeans and shirt. They must have hit him again because he had that coppery taste in his mouth. He stared up at a black sky, picked himself up. Tommy stared at each of them. He fished out his wallet and looked inside, then closed it.

"It's your lucky day, Jimmy," Tommy said. "Looks like I got your money after all. Here." When Tommy threw the wallet to Jimmy, he withdrew a pair of brass knuckles from his jacket pocket. He slipped his fingers through the holes.

He didn't wait for Jimmy to catch the wallet. Tommy turned on Pete first. He swung him around fast, delivered combinations to the body. Tommy heard Pete's ribs give, or at least some of them. Then he threw an uppercut with the knuckles. Pete's jaw made a snapping noise. Pete dropped to the alley floor. Fast.

Tommy turned to face Jimmy and Malcolm. He made quick work of them both. Tommy planted two powerful blows to Jimmy's throat, only because he once threatened Tommy's mother. Blood spurted in large gouts out of Jimmy's mouth and nose. His teeth went away. Tommy knocked one of Malcolm's eyes so far back in his head, he thought maybe Malcolm might catch a glimpse of his own brain.

Now Tommy stood over all three men. He picked up his wallet, shook off the water. "Tell you what," Tommy said. "I'll get you your money, Jimmy. But you come around this way again lookin' for trouble, I'll hand your ass to you. Got it?" Course Jimmy had nothing to offer. He lay on the alley floor unconscious. Malcolm had crawled to the opposite wall. He pulled himself up slowly. Tommy could not see his eye. "You finished?"

Malcolm waved a hand. "I'm-I'm done, man. No more."

Tommy said, "Good. That's real good. You give Jimmy the message when he wakes up. The other one, too. You come back inside I'll kill all three of you. Clear?"

Tommy walked back inside. He motioned for the barkeep. "Keep em comin' for a while, huh, Dale." After seven shots, Tommy could hardly keep his head up. His head swam worse than ever. He packed it in and walked home.

The next morning, Tommy rolled out of bed. He ran to the bathroom and vomited, brushed his teeth, cleaned up. Looking in the mirror, he wondered if some ribs got mashed. He could not remember the fight at Chick's last night.

He left the bedroom and put on some boiled eggs, downed half a bottle of wine before the shakes ebbed. The shakes and the vomiting had become a part of him. Tommy ate the eggs and finished the bottle of wine, walked into the bedroom. He saw a badly wrinkled sheaf of paper on the floor. He read the inscription:

Saw you fight tonight. Meet me at 2253 Lincoln Street at 1:00 AM. Get some rest. Stay off the liquor until we talk. 25,000 dollars in it for you if you win.

Funny how the guy watched him fight last night and Tommy couldn't remember the last time he'd pissed. Tommy ignored the *stay off the liquor* thing, and drove down to the liquor store and bought a gallon of whiskey. About five he passed out. When he awoke it was 12:30 AM.

Shit!

He found the place easy enough. The street was dark. The buildings abandoned. He pulled the Nova to the curb, cut the engine. A moment later he saw movement outside 2253. The building was tall and made of brick. Tommy approached the man cautiously.

"Morning," said the man. The stranger held a scratch-off ticket in his hand. He didn't look up as he scratched the ticket feverishly. He blew the silver residue off the card, pitched it to the sidewalk.

"You win some, you lose some."

"You the man left me the note?"

"Edward," said the man.

He was a Puerto Rican fellow with short black hair. He

sported a jean jacket and blue jeans. They shook hands.

"Why the note?"

"Because last night. You fight three men. All three went down," said Edward smiling. "Amazing show. So I talk to you a little at bar. You drunk so I write note for you. I see you didn't lose it, no."

"The note said $25,000 if I win."

"Yes."

"Yes?"

"You smell like shit-heap and vomit," said Edward. "Too much drink. Follow."

Tommy followed Edward into an alley. They walked a while without talking.

"Look this," Edward said after fishing coupons out of his pocket. "America. Deals every day. Look here." He held one up. "Burger King Value Meals. This other for supermarket. So many savings. I make my wife happy. I go buy porterhouse steaks later this morning. Cook her big breakfast. No deals where I come from. No Salvation Army. No thrift stores. We come to America six year ago. We had nothing. Then Mr. Bunker find me and offer me a job. Pay is good. Fighters get more."

"Fighters?"

"You have job, yes?"

"Between jobs right now."

"How you pay rent?"

"I manage."

"You manage?" Edward dug into his pocket again, fished out a roll of twenties, and licked his thumb. "How much rent?"

"That's not necessary," Tommy said. "I get by."

"You get by nothing. How much?"

"Two fifty."

Edward handed Tommy the money. He counted out more. "Get food, too."

"Thanks." Tommy shoved the money into his pocket. "You mentioned fighters," Tommy said. "What is this place?"

"You see."

Tommy and Edward approached a metal door on the side

of the building. Edward knocked. A square sheet of thin metal slid open.

"Yeah?" came a voice from inside.

"Edward. Got new fighter."

The door opened.

Edward and Tommy stepped inside.

"This is Leo," Edward said. "Leo, this is Tommy. He man I told you about."

Leo must've been the biggest black man Tommy'd ever seen. Leo loomed over Tommy with a quizzical look.

"Don't look like much," Leo said. "Bunker see 'em yet?"

"Not yet. He will. Trust me. This one wins, no problem. Promise. We get his opponent out of ring for good. Man scares me."

"Evening," Tommy said to the giant. The giant said nothing.

"Come," said Edward. He shuffled Tommy away down several flights of stairs. "I show you."

Was about the fifth stairwell when the stink hit Tommy. He heaved, turned away from it.

"Jesus H. Christ!"

"I know," said Edward. "It get better. Well, not better. You get use to it. We share next to sewer. It's other side of wall where I taking you. Come."

Tommy reluctantly followed.

"Who the hell am I supposed to fight? Who were you talking about?"

Edward opened a door on the 8th stairwell and they walked inside. A steady drum filtered through what looked like a tunnel. Rats scuttled along in the darkness. Edward pulled a flashlight out of his inside jean's coat. He flicked it on.

"Not until fight night. Fighters don't know who they fighting until fight night. Mr. Bunker likes it that way," Edward said. "Here. This way."

"What's that noise? The drumming?"

"Fight's tonight. They fight every night. Sounds like big crowd. Mr. Bunker be happy. Much money be made."

"Twenty-five thousand?" asked Tommy.

"If you win."

A stream of brown murky water swept passed them. Rats rode atop the water on floating garbage. They scuttled about everywhere. Edward kicked them out of their path and into the water.

"We here," Edward said. "You be excited when you see."

"I'm fighting tonight?"

"Next weekend."

"Oh?"

"Get rest."

Edward opened another door. They stepped inside. Cheers erupted nearby. Edward flicked his flashlight off, tucked it away, and opened another door which led into a brightly lit room.

Tommy didn't exactly know what to say. Cigarette smoke hung heavy in the underground arena. Two men in the center of the room pummeled each other.

"Mr. Bunker call it cage fighting."

One of the fighters gave an elbow to his opponent's forehead. Blood came in thick gouts, blanketing the mat beneath them. The bleeding fighter staggered backward blindly and fell. They grappled, blood bathing over both of them.

"Is it one of them I'm fighting?" asked Tommy.

"Maybe one day it be real sport in America," said Edward. "And no. He don't fight every night. One fight a week. Next weekend you fight him."

Tommy looked on in amazement. He said, "Looks more like cockfighting to me. This legal?"

Edward smiled. "Come. You see enough. I take you back up."

Tommy sat in his car staring out at the dark streets. "Who am I fighting?" asked Tommy. "Least you can do is tell me that."

Edward stood outside the car, breathing in the city air. "Can't. Mr. Bunker be upset I tell you. Fighter very scary, Tommy. He know I tell, he send him my place to break my bones. Not good."

"You can't be serious?"

"I am," said Edward. "Get rest this week. Much to do next weekend."

Tommy stopped off at the liquor store, bought a pint of whiskey, then headed home. When he got there he found Ellen dozing on the couch. Ellen lived upstairs. They'd been dating about a year now. She heard him come in and sat up.

"Tommy?"

"It's me."

"Where you been?" she asked sleepily.

"Out," Tommy said. He poured two whiskies and gave her a glass.

"Is it someone else?"

"Nothing like that. Got a job."

"Oh?"

"Yeah."

"Doing what?"

"Fighting."

"Fighting," Ellen snapped. "You're forty years old. And what happened to your face?"

"Mixed it up with a few guys down at the bar last night," Tommy said. He finished his glass, poured another.

"Have you gone mad? You can't fight."

"No, I've gone broke. Twenty-five thousand if I win." Tommy poured another drink. "And yes I am."

Ellen pulled up her blouse, smiling. "My man the fighter." Tommy's cock stiffened as he put down his glass and undressed. He took her right there on the couch. She never wore panties. A good thing. He slid his shaft inside her. She was warm and wet. Ellen moaned. Sweat trailed down between her breasts, which Tommy eagerly lapped up. She gripped his back, fingernails digging in. He pushed her legs over her head and slammed it to her hard. She withered beneath him as she dug her nails into his chest. Both of them sweating and grunting and moving as one.

"Goddammit!"

"That's it, baby," Tommy released, pulled out. He looked into her eyes, kissed her forehead, her cheek. Tommy got up, dressed and mopped hair out of his eyes, then turned on the fan.

"Swear," Ellen said, gasping for breath, "you're the best I've ever had." She was touching herself. Her face glistened with sweat. "How do you do it? I mean, shit, you've never lasted long, but you sure can-"

"Cause I'm the best, baby," Tommy said as he walked into the kitchen. He boiled some eggs to go with the rest of the whiskey.

Ellen left the couch and stood under the archway. "Who is it?"

"Who's what?"

"Who're you fighting? You must know."

"I don't. Little guy wouldn't tell me."

"Can I come?"

"Not that kind of place, baby," Tommy said. "Better not. Place stinks. It's an underground thing. I've seen it. Real nasty."

"It won't kill me to go. You won't even know I'm there. There's someone else, isn't there?" Ellen's fists clenched. "Bastard!"

"There's no one else."

"You've told me that before."

"I'm serious this time."

"I wanna come."

"You just did."

"Dammit, Tommy!"

"Stop it," he said. "The answer's no. Too dangerous." Jesus was it bad. Rats. The smell. The whole underground thing astonished him. "Tell the truth, the place scared the shit outta me."

"I hate you."

"You love my cock."

"There is that."

"Look, baby, I need to rest. You stay I'll end up fucking you again. Go on upstairs. I need to sleep. Edward told me to get some rest. Can't do it with you here. He fished out the money Edward had given him and handed her some. "Go to the store. Get some food. Bring me back some of that fine wine—the good stuff. We'll fix something tomorrow."

"So there's no one else?"

"No. I promise," Tommy said. "Now go. I got to sleep."

The next day Ellen returned with two bottles of red wine— the good stuff. She carried a brown paper bag.

"What's in the other bag?" asked Tommy, opening one of the bottles.

"It's a surprise."

"I hate surprises."

"I know," Ellen said. "It's for later."

They drank their wine and ate their dinner and by early evening they were in bed. Tommy saw the paper bag on the chest of drawers.

"Gonna tell me what it is?"

Ellen opened the bag, pulled out three tubes. "Sex paint," she said excitedly.

Tommy liked simple. He struggled with change. Change was never a good thing. At night he drew the blinds and locked the doors—sometimes checking and rechecking them numerous times before he was content. And he lived his little existence as if he had no neighbors. Fixed in his ways. Nothing, as far as he knew, would ever change that. All this drove Ellen bug-shit. Yet she dealt with his insanities the only way she knew how—by ignoring it.

She sat on the bed. She squeezed some of the red paint out on her finger. "It's edible too. Here," she said touching his lips.

Tommy licked some off his lips, only to watch Ellen suck the rest off her finger. Tommy didn't mind the taste. He liked it a lot. Tasted like strawberries.

"What're you going to do with it?"

"This." She painted Tommy's cock with it. She rubbed it on real good. She was about to take him in her mouth when someone knocked on the door. "Be right back." She dressed and ran from the room. A second later she was back, eyes wild.

"Who is it?" asked Tommy.

"My parents."

"Your parents?" Tommy flung himself off the bed, headed for the bathroom.

"Where you going?"

"Take a shower. Get this shit off me."

"Never mind that. Get dressed. Forgot I told them that if I wasn't home to come down here. They're early."

"Perfect."

The paint was thick. It squished against Tommy's upper inner thigh. "I should wash it off at least."

"Forget it. You'll be fine. They won't stay long." And with that she was out of the room. Tommy heard the chatter of greetings and hugs and laughter.

Tommy found Ellen's father sitting in the living room, cross legged and staring at nothing. The girls were in the kitchen.

"Afternoon, Ted," Tommy said. He'd met them only once last year during a New Year's Eve party Ellen put together. "Drink?"

"Sounds nice, Tommy, thanks."

Tommy poured two glasses of wine, handed one to Ted. "How's the work coming?"

"Slow. Money filters in when I need it." Tommy saw the disappointment on Ted's face. "It'll come."

Ted finished his glass and poured another. "Sooner than later I hope."

An hour into their visit the sex paint began to harden.

Tommy found movement limited. The hardened paint tightened with each shift or reposition in his seat. The paint found his pubic hair, tangled all up in there, tightened down like a vice. The head of his cock stuck to his underwear. *Jesus! This can't be happening. I should kill Ellen for this. Don't wash it off, she said. It'll be fine, she said. Thank God I don't have a boner or—*

Ellen's mother walked in. She wore a short black skirt. Her blouse hung open just enough to catch a glimpse of her milky white breasts, and when she leaned over to shake Tommy's hand, her blouse opened further. Tommy looked down her shirt, noted her stiffened, pink nipples. For an older lady, she was damn hot. Tommy squirmed in his seat. A scream almost erupted deep down in the cavity of his guts.

"Sorry for not seeing you, Tommy. Nice to see you again."

"Something wrong, Tommy?" Ted poured another drink.

"I'm fine," Tommy said. "Little under the weather is all. Ellen came down to check on me."

"Well," Ellen's mother said, "maybe we should leave. Ted?"

"Nonsense," Ellen said striding into the room. "He'll be fine."

Bitch!

Tommy gave her a look unlike anything Ellen had ever seen.

"But maybe you should go upstairs just in case. Never know, could be the flu or something."

Tommy stood under the shower for what seemed like a lifetime; scrubbing and plucking thick, wet chunks of red paint out of his pubes and off his nut sack.

"Thought you said this shit was cool?" Tommy lathered up a fresh batch of suds. "I'm so raw and red; it's hard to tell what's paint and what isn't."

"I'm sorry, baby." Ellen handed him a clear plastic Ziploc bag.

"Oh, good." Tommy shut off the water, stepped out of the tub. He toweled off, took the bag, and opened it. He grabbed up a handful and applied the powdery softness. Heaven was brief. Tommy's nether region turned into an inferno. "Jesus! Fuck!" he said as he swept his hand down to rub the powder off. The powder stuck. "Goddammit, Ellen." Tommy tripped backward into the tub. He scrambled to his feet, turned the water on. A cold blast of spray hit him in the chest. It wasn't getting warmer. Tommy knew what it was Ellen had given him: baking soda.

Tommy doctored up his manhood with the corn starch. Then he had Ellen run down to the corner store for more whiskey. Since fucking was out of the question, he got drunk and passed out. When he awoke, Ellen was gone.

The week went by without incident. In the underground locker room, Tommy sat on a table, feet dangling over a warped and badly cracked cement floor that'd seen better days. Lenny, a short pudgy man of about 72 walked into the room, a towel draped over one shoulder. His face puffy and red, his nose mashed nearly flat to his face. He walked with a slight hobble.

Lenny tossed the towel on the table next to Tommy. "Let's get those hands taped."

"Who am I fighting?"

"You'll see soon enough," Lenny said. "First the hands. Hold 'em out."

Tommy did. Lenny wrapped.

"Glad you showed," Lenny said. "Got a lot of money on this. So does the crowd out there. Way Edward tells it, you got a helluva right hook. Said you took three guys at once down at Chick's last week. How are you feelin'?"

"Fine," Tommy said. "These locker rooms always smell like piss?"

"Yes. You will get used to it. We all do. Well, those of us who live down here. A lot of fighters, kid, have come and gone. Some have even died in this very room. But not you. No, sir. You're gonna do us all a favor and cream this sumbitch." Lenny finished Tommy's right hand, and then moved over to the left. Tommy opened his hand palm down.

"I've never fought in a cage before," Tommy confessed. "Feels odd."

His stomach began to knot up at the sound of the crowd in the arena.

"Never mind that. Fighting is fighting. You stay away from his blows. You hear? Do what you got to do, but don't let him land a punch."

"That powerful, huh?"

Lenny cringed as he finished taping Tommy's right hand. "Got nothin' to do with power, kid. Here, hold out your arms." Tommy did. Lenny ran his callused hands up Tommy's arms, massaging them. "Listen. You listening to me?"

"Yeah."

"You get to him first. Combinations. Jabs. Work on the body, break a few ribs soon as you can. But don't let him touch you. Careful with his arm bar. Seen 'em break several arms with that one."

"How the hell am I supposed to do that? Run around the ring?"

"Just you listen." Lenny snatched up the towel he'd thrown on the table. He threw it across his shoulder. "Things are different down here in the underground, kid. Rules don't apply. Not with him. Not ever. Hear? You got sand. A whole damn lot. But there comes a time you got to have more than sand. This guy is mean."

"Who the hell am I fighting?"

"You'll find out soon enough."

The crowd roared, filling the catacombs of the underground

as Tommy slid from the table. He danced and jigged and punched the air.

Lenny slipped the gloves on Tommy, said, "Don't you be getting all confident. He's fought twelve times. Six died right in this room."

"You can't be serious!"

"Yep. And things ain't been right since he come. Not right at all. Spectators thought it was neat having him here. Then things turned dark. Like I said, don't let him hit you. Not even once."

"I don't understand."

"Bad things happen when he hits his opponents."

"I'm sure it does. Broken nose. Ribs—"

"Stop laughing!"

"Be cool, Lenny. I got this."

"You got shit," Lenny said. "Others have said the same thing. They didn't. Listen. Every time he hits you, things come out of the dark. Nasty things. For instance, last time he fought a fellow named Jones. Jones damn near tore the guy's jaw right the hell off, but the guy recovered and came back with a massive uppercut. Bats came down out of the dark when that happened. God only knows where they came from. WHAM! And they were on him. Seconds later they ripped that poor bastard all to hell and back. Wasn't much left of 'em. He died right here in this room. Right on this table."

The door to the locker room opened. In walked a man close to Lenny's age, tall with short cropped hair and balding on top. Despite the heat, the man wore a dark blue three-piece suit, and aided by a walking cane made of marble.

Edward followed close behind, scratching off a ticket with a coin. He grumbled something, and tossed the ticket on the floor. He wore the same clothes he'd worn last week. The old man with the cane looked Tommy over, head to toe, then smiled.

"Mighty fine, mighty fine."

"Mr. Bunker, sir," Lenny said.

Mr. Bunker nodded. "Lenny." He looked to Tommy. "Nice of you to show, Mr. Morris. Glad I didn't bet against you. Guess that twenty five-thousand got you thinking, huh?"

"It helped," Tommy said.

"You no smell like shit-heap and vomit," Edward said.

"Well," Tommy stared coldly at Edward, "at least I do have other clothes." This went over Edward's head. He didn't mention Edward's smell either.

"Enough, guys," Lenny warned. "We're almost ready, Mr. Bunker. Few more minutes."

"Take your time. Crowd won't be walking out tonight. Not with *him* fighting they won't."

"What is this place?" asked Tommy.

"Whatever you want it to be," Bunker said. "We call it the underground. Two fighters go in the cage, one fighter wins."

"Or one dies," Lenny said. Mr. Bunker wrinkled his nose.

Bunker strolled over to the sink, leaned against it, and faced Tommy. "It does happen, Tommy. Listen to Lenny here. He's old school. Fought bare knuckles back in the day. I don't know, maybe one day we won't have to fight in a place like this. I call it MMA. I see it being a major sport in the future. Much like boxing only more blood and skill."

"I saw a little last week," Tommy said.

"You called it what?"

"He call it cockfighting, Mr. Bunker," Edward sneered.

Amused, Bunker grinned and said, "I like MMA much better, Tommy. Sounds professional.

The door swung open. A man wearing black trunks with red stripes stepped inside. He stood every bit at 6'5, hair gray and parted down the middle. He held a paperback in one gloved hand.

"That him?" The man crossed his arms against his bare chest. At first Tommy thought this was a joke. To think this was the undisputed champ amazed him. "They call me The Butcher."

"This him," Edward said matter-of-factly. Mr. Bunker stepped away from the men.

Lenny got between Butcher and Tommy. "You can't be in here. It's not time yet."

"He doesn't look like much," The Butcher said.

"Dynamite comes in small packages, Butcher," Bunker said.

"I'm saving myself," said Tommy. "Ain't nothin' but a thing.

I take you and walk away twenty-five thousand dollars richer."
The guy looked familiar. He'd seen him before. Tommy was
almost sure of it. Could he have been in pictures? The old horror
movies of yesteryear? Damn if he could not remember.

"Ain't?" The Butcher's face reddened. "I should give you a
beat down right here for the bad grammar, you little twat."

"Out, Butcher," Lenny snapped. "Take it up with him in the
cage. You know the rules."

"Sure do," Butcher said. "There *ain't* none."

With that The Butcher left the room.

Lenny continued Tommy's rub down. A rat scuttled past
them. None of the men flinched. The crowd died down in the
arena.

"He must have gone in," Lenny said.

"How you know?" asked Tommy

"They fear him," Mr. Bunker said. "This ends tonight." He
pointed at all of them. "You hear me, Tommy? I want him out
of the underground tonight. Don't care what you do, or how
it goes down, but you win tonight. You win, he leaves. Wasn't
but about a few years ago I put out a hit on him. Guy ran him
down with his van. Bastard was so looped by the time he found
The Butcher he called the paramedics. Sat on a fuckin' stump
and called for help. Wasn't long after that the authorities found
my hired man in his house—what was left of him—eaten by
his own dogs. Would have been done with him then wasn't for
that drunken asshole. Lucky for me The Butcher didn't put two
and two together." Bunker checked his watch and said, "We
better get on out there. About that time. You ready?" Bunker
eyed Tommy.

"I got this," Tommy said.

"Good."

They left the locker room.

The arena mirrored an ancient Roman coliseum. Torches
lined the walls like some medieval torture chamber. The room
was circular with wide cement seats, which were smooth and
blended seamlessly together. The ring, known as the cage, sat
at its center. A vaulted ceiling went so far up Tommy could not
see the inner dome. The Butcher waited inside the cage reading

his paperback. When he saw Tommy he grumbled something and tossed the paperback onto the mat.

The crowd exploded with cheers and chants as Tommy made his way toward the cage.

"Jesus." Tommy took everything in. His heart thumped heavily in his chest. He felt light on his feet.

"It's all for you," Bunker said. "They've been waiting for someone strong enough to take him down. Like I said back in the locker room, Tommy, this ends tonight. Get him outta here."

"I'll do my best, Mr. Bunker." Tommy got inside the cage. The crowd was so deafening now that he could barely hear Edward wishing him luck.

Tommy and The Butcher squared off. The crowd died down to a whisper. Both fighters circled the cage. Neither man threw a punch. Not at first.

Tommy glanced to Lenny, who stood just outside the cage. *'You get to him first. Combinations. Jabs. Work on the body, break a few ribs soon as you can. But don't let him touch you.'* Tommy remembered Lenny's stone advice, and moved fast, unloading body shots and combinations one after another. The Butcher's eyes went wild in their sockets as blow after blow connected. The Butcher toppled over in a mess of limbs, regained his footing and charged, swinging violently. Tommy easily sidestepped the assault and opened up with his own arsenal of maneuvers, which The Butcher was ready for.

Wish I'd been able to use my brass knuckles, Tommy thought as he watched The Butcher pivot on his right foot. Tommy did the same. The Butcher threw a wild right hook that almost connected. The crowd, cheering and chanting Tommy's name, now stood on their feet. The coliseum thundered all around them. Tommy thought he heard Lenny, but waved him off like a troublesome mosquito.

The Butcher moved to the right and left, then delivered an unmerciful jab that rocked Tommy backward a few steps.

The crowd went silent as Tommy circled The Butcher.

"Now's when the fun starts, kiddo," The Butcher said with a grin. He relaxed. He paced the mat leisurely. A deep, guttural snarl filled the coliseum then, as if something were chewing its way up through the mat.

"Hear it?" asked The Butcher. "You should have left while you had the chance, Tommy."

And then the mat tore out from under Tommy's feet. He fell through the canvas. Darkness greeted him beneath the cage. But the darkness did not scare him half as much as what waited in the gloom, because it now circled him, sizing him up, closing the gap.

Steel beams crisscrossed under the cage, holding the structure intact. A single shaft of light spilled through the opening where Tommy had fallen through. His eyes adjusted to the dark in time to see the beast stalking him, a wolf with thick bristled fur which was matted down with what looked like dried blood.

"Jesus!" Tommy stumbled backward on his haunches as it closed the gap.

"*Ain't* nothin' but a thing, right, Tommy," The Butcher said mockingly from above. "That *is* what you said, correct?" It was, Tommy knew. He regretted saying it now. In truth, he regretted this whole thing. Broke or not, he wanted out. But how? *Don't care what you do, or how it goes down, but you win tonight.* Bunker's words rang true. *No rules, right?* Tommy thought.

Tommy slipped between the metal beams to distance himself. He looked for something to mash its head, found nothing, moved and slithered clumsily among the supports. At one point he thought he might make it back to the opening in which he'd fell through, but that wasn't to be. The wolf gained, bore down on him, reached out with a quick slap. Claws opened Tommy's back.

Tommy screamed.

The wolf howled. Its prey wounded, it moved in for the kill. It slammed into one of the beams. Two supports broke. The cage off kilter, Tommy heard metal clatter on the concrete floor. The whole of the cage tilted. And it was close. He saw it. Part of the metal beam had come loose when the wolf collided with the structure. A nine inch piece about three feet away lay with its end peeled back, leaving a sharpened edge. Tommy scrambled for it. The wolf must have noticed because it came on fast.

Tommy reached it first. He picked up the weapon and rolled

onto his back as the wolf pounced. He brought up the metal shank, impaling the beast. The wolf howled and vanished. Tommy didn't waste any time. He scrambled up and out of the hole where The Butcher greeted him at the opening.

The crowd roared.

"Imagine that," The Butcher said. "I didn't see that coming. Wise move." Tommy gained his feet. The Butcher did not see the shaft in Tommy's hand as he advanced on Tommy.

"Thought that was wise?" Tommy said as he waited for his move, remembering what Lenny had told him about the man who gave The Butcher his first hammering uppercut. "You should see this one."

The Butcher didn't have time to stop. He saw the shaft too late as Tommy came up with an uppercut, driving the nine inch shaft home. The Butcher grabbed at his throat.

The crowd cheered.

The Butcher's arms dropped to his sides as blood flowed down his chest. His legs buckled. Tommy watched him fall to the mat, body convulsing, shriveling up. His flesh softened to the point it dripped off bone, mixed with the onrush of blood blanketing the mat. Then The Butcher was gone in a haze of smoke.

Tommy looked around at the spectators, then to Lenny, Edward, and Mr. Bunker.

"Get my money," Tommy said.

Bunker's office was nothing like Tommy imagined. Lenny and Edward stood near the door while Bunker sat behind an expensive cherry wood desk. Bookshelves lined all four walls. The carpet was pearl white. Two table lamps sat in each corner behind Bunker.

"Nice job tonight, Tommy," Bunker said. "I'm pleased."

"My money, Mr. Bunker," Tommy said. "And I'll be on my way. I've smelled enough of this place."

Bunker smiled, opened a drawer. He tossed a manila envelope on the desk.

"You've earned it rightfully, Tommy."

"Yes he has," Lenny agreed. "He fight again, Mr. Bunker?"

Tommy took the envelope, swiveled around in his chair with a wince. Quick movements caused him to lose his breath.

"Those stitches'll hold about two, three weeks, Tommy," Lenny said.

"Thanks, Lenny." Tommy stood, pocketing the money. "I'm retired, Edward. No more for me. I came to do what I came to do."

"Are you sure, Tommy?" Bunker said. "I mean twenty-five thousand a fight isn't change, friend."

Tommy waved him off. He started for the door. Lenny and Edward made a path.

"You ever need money, Tommy, you know how to make it."

"Yes, I do," Tommy said. "Punching a clock is a lot less painful."

On the way home Tommy thought about Ellen. Maybe it was time to bring up the big question. After all, they've been dating a year now. Sex was great, though he could do without the sex paint. Never again, he thought. Never again. It wasn't until tonight during the fight that he'd realized how much he *did* love her. *'I'll be right here when you get back. You win it for us, baby. It's as bad as you say, I'll stay here. But you win. Hear?'* With the money he made tonight, they could get married; even take that trip to Colorado, a place they've both wanted to visit. For the first time in his life the future seemed brighter—clearer than ever before. To share it with Ellen only seemed right. Hell, he could stop by the jewelry store in the morning and buy the biggest rock they offered. Forty wasn't so old, and Ellen was only twenty-seven. Still in her prime.

The one lane bridge came into view ahead.

Tommy was thinking about how to propose to Ellen when a pair of high beams flooded the interior of the Nova from behind. It jolted his thoughts. He slowed to let the car pass. It didn't. Instead the vehicle rolled up alongside the Nova. Though he knew it was there, Tommy did not look. He kept on. Almost to the bridge, the car swung hard to the right. Metal racked against metal. Tommy yelped in fear, and wondered if Jimmy Coulter, Ralph Randal, and Pete Malcolm hadn't decided to collect their money after all. The car came in again, this time harder, knocking the Nova nearly off the road.

"Hey!" Tommy shouted. His rear tire hit the ditch. Losing traction, the Nova spun its tires and nearly slid sidelong off into the gully as Tommy fought to regain control. It did not help.

The car came in a second time.

Before Tommy and the Nova spilled over the ledge of the hundred and fifty foot gully, Tommy saw the car in his headlights. A 1958 Plymouth Fury. There was no one driving.

THE WALLET

Randy Norton drove home beaten and bloody. He ran his hand down the left side of his face and it came away sticky and red. His left eye swollen shut, nose crushed against his face, his upper lip dangled down over his bottom lip like a thick loose hair. Perhaps it was the shock holding the pain hostage. Damn, Randy thought, I'm a real mess.

At three o'clock in the morning, traffic wasn't hectic. Lights blinked yellow through town. Front of his shirt clung to his chest. He'd wet it down to get the blood to soften. Part time job? Did he need it? Shit. He almost wanted to cry, but that'd only blur his vision. A possible pull over by police he could do without.

Randy turned onto a snow-covered drive, which led half a mile out into the wild. No one lived out this far. Isolated by thick forest on all sides, he approached his house. He pulled to a stop and cut the engine. A barn owl called out some place in the woods.

Inside the house was cold and dark. He gathered wood and built a fire. Then he walked upstairs to his room and lit a few candles. He slipped his pants off, pissed in a five gallon bucket beside the bed, and then set about looking for the needle and thread Betty had kept handy. He found them in a top dresser drawer Betty had kept around. He never knew why. The drawers were coming apart and some of them, if you pulled on them too hard, the knobs would come off. No clothes inside, just whatever. He returned to the small dresser (make-up desk he called it; Betty knew the correct name) and stared at the creature in the mirror. Randy waited for his hands to stop shaking, then threaded the string through the eyehole, bent the needle, tied his hair back in a ponytail and went to work on his mangled face.

Wind outside kicked up. A frosty sheet of ice glazed the windows. The weather forecast promised five inches of snow by tomorrow night. *Hadn't we had enough?* He saw his breath as he began to thread the string through soft swollen flesh.

As he worked the needle, he noticed the pink puffiness of the open abrasion down his cheek. Another battle scar under my belt, he thought. He'd never been this close to death. Death, the asshole that he was, had walked up and shook his hand tonight.

"Lost a little of your good looks tonight, old boy," Randy said. *What would Betty have done? She'd sew you up good as new and kiss it afterward, that's what. If only he'd gone to the store that night, she'd still be alive. And what about you? Screw me. Should have been me in the car that night.*

Three years ago a trip to the store took Betty out of his life forever. 'Course she'd driven the same road the past twenty years. She knew it well. The deer did not. It had come out of the dark and shot across the road. Randy had seen it when police drove him to the scene. What he'd walked up on still haunted him. Local yokels called it a one in a million chance. The deer, a large fourteen point buck, crashed through the windshield of the Honda Civic and took her completely by surprise. She didn't even brake for it. Its antlers severed her head completely. That's when he had decided to let himself go. Stop paying the bills. Live off the land.

Randy put down the needle. He checked out his work. Not bad, but not good either. His lip curled up in a mangled snarl from the thread. He knew the chances of coming out of this not looking like Elvis was slim to none.

He left the needle and went downstairs. He stoked the fire, threw on another log. Then he gathered more wood, spread out a few blankets, and lay down. He almost called in at his full-time job at American Railcar but thought better of it. He needed the cash. The part-time gig could suck his cock.

Sleep came and threw him back into the alley from which

he'd crawled, only now death was pissed and raging and wanted his soul.

And the wallet he fought to keep.

"Shit," Joel said.

"What?" Pickle said.

"They're melting early today." Joel rested the tanks near the railcar, unwound the cutting torch line, and opened the valves. He sniffed the air. "Almost here, man. I can almost smell it. No breeze all week, now it kicks up in our direction."

The Rendering Plant started the ovens. Down a short dirt road from American Railcar, white smoke ate away at the blue sky.

The Rendering Plant melted down roadkill on Tuesdays and Fridays. The stockyards fed most of the plant regularly. Each morning on his drive in, Joel usually had to steer around a dead cow or hog delivered to the stockyards. Most times the livestock was dead. Other times they might have eaten too much and couldn't move through the gates and into their stalls, so they'd just lay there. The night watchman of the yard would then go out and plug them in the head with a shotgun. Jesse James slept the night in one of those old stalls, so the place became an historical landmark. Truth to tell it probably made the Rendering Plant happy.

The smell hadn't hit the welding shop so far, but it was slowly driving closer. Nothing could be done about it. You wanted a job you dealt with the stench. Even if the rail shop didn't pay much, it put food on the table, and that's all Joel needed.

"You see Randy this morning?" Pickel asked. "Looks like he got the shit kicked outta him something bad over the weekend. Never saw him get it like this."

Pickel, aka Jerry Strut, got his name on account he ate dill pickles all day long. One for first break, four for lunch, and one before going home.

"Didn't see. Must've just missed 'em," Joel said.

"All the other guys went quiet and shit when he clocked in. Randy got his paperwork and shuffled over to his railcar. Man, he got it bad. Face is all busted up. Didn't say a word to no one."

"Car accident, maybe?" Joel said. "Can't see him getting whipped big as he is."

"Me neither," Pickel said.

"Out of all the jobs here, this is my least favorite. Hate cutting walk boards. It's almost like a demotion. Rather be welding. Know I'm good at cutting them off, but shit…"

Pickel threw his line up on top of the railcar next to Joel's and said, "Yeah, well, at least you don't have to haul this fucker up by a rope." He pointed down at his TIG welder. "Wanna switch?"

"Nah. I got this. Hate being downwind from the place and up twenty two feet in the air, damn near knocks you out. Glad I got a strong stomach."

Joel Newman climbed up onto his assigned job of cutting old walk boards off the railcars' roofs and replacing them with new ones. A master of the cutting torch, Joel proved himself a worthy craftsman of the trade.

Out of ten hired last month, he was the last. Twenty two and straight out of school, Joel had something the other nine didn't have: a strong stomach and experience. Contaminated metal can be a bitch if you've never welded on it. Fortunately for Joel he could weld just about anything under his hood. Not too many could say that at his age. His father had taught him the art years before he graduated with a Class A certificate from the university. Once he watched his father weld two bubblegum wrappers together. It was the most impressive thing he'd ever witnessed.

Flash burn at the age of ten almost caused him to give up welding, but his father laid him in bed, and taped two rounded slices of potato over his eyes. Wasn't but about five hours later he rose from bed and removed the potatoes. Both slices had turned coal black.

"Sucks out the heat," his father had said.

Though his eyes continued to feel as if someone had poured sand into them, much of the agony had ebbed. Mostly. Sunglasses for a week came in handy.

The morning went on. Southern Pacific dropped off two more grain cars to add to the workload.

"Hey."

Joel looked up from cutting walk boards, "What?"

"Need a favor," Pickel said.

"Yeah?"

"Go down and tell Randy I need a few things from him."

Joel pulled off his cutting goggles and leather heat gloves. "What you need?"

"Slag hammer, welding lens... and ask him how his dad does push-ups."

Joel said, "I'm not asking him that. You're crazier than a shit-house rat you think I'm askin' him that. You said he was all busted up this morning."

Randy stood all of six eight and came in about two hundred and ninety.

"He ain't gonna say nuttin'," Pickle said. "Go on."

"Hell's bells."

"C'mon, man."

"Okay."

Joel found Randy in the shop welding beneath a grain car. A torpedo heater blasted close to him. Sparks exploded as he welded overhead, one of the more difficult welds to master. Some had it, some didn't. Aside from his own father, Randy was one of the best he'd ever seen.

"Randy?"

Randy didn't stop working. His voice was muffled under his hood. Something in his voice didn't sound right, like his mouth was packed with cotton. "What is it?"

"Jerry needs a few things from ya."

He stopped welding, rolled out from under the railcar, and took off his hood.

Joel grimaced, turned his head. Left side of Randy's face looked as if someone'd bounced a brick off it repeatedly. And for days. One eye was so damaged he couldn't open it. His nose, in no better condition, lay flat against his face. His upper lip was mashed and stitched. Whoever stitched him up must've been working fast or didn't know jack about the job. His lip curled upward leaving his teeth and gum exposed.

"What does he need now?" Randy grumbled. "Got to fix

this before lunch. Pacific's picking it up this afternoon."

"Hell happened to your face, Randy?" It all came rolling out before Joel could put the brakes on.

"Go ahead," said a man walking past. "What did happen? Weren't like that last week."

"Shut it, Jimmy," Randy said, 'fore I dump a bucket of water under you next I see you weldin'."

It was a standing joke. The old dumping of the water under a man welding. Kind of causes a fella to do the jig a bit when the welding machine is grounded to the railcar. Won't kill you, but it'll sure light you up fast.

"Never you mind my face, boy," Randy said. "What's Pickel want?"

"Told me he needs a slag hammer and new lens. Oh, and, can you tell me how your dad does push-ups?"

For a moment Randy said nothing. He didn't have to. His face turned beet red. He clenched his ham-sized hands into cannonball fists. He stepped forward and grabbed Joel by his shirt. He pulled him in close.

"Listen here, new fish," Randy said. "You tell that Pickel fuckin' sumbitch he never gave back my hammer last time. Ain't seen it. Broke the last two lenses I gave him three weeks ago. Don't take care of nothin', that little bastard. You mind what I say. Don't lend 'em nothin' you don't want gone or broken. And the shit about my daddy?"

"Listen, Randy, I was—"

"Daddy lost his arms in Nam, new fish. Got it? He can't so much as wipe his own ass."

Joel wanted to crawl under a rock, a railcar slithering with vipers, anything to take him away from the giant that held him now. "Man, I didn't know."

Men working nearby roared with laughter.

Randy smirked. He slapped Joel's cheek playfully.

"Thought I was gonna do you right here, didn't ya?"

"Enough to damn near make me crap," Joel said, letting out a long breath.

"You new fish fall for that all the time. Knew you was gonna be stickin' round. Other boys you come in with didn't know what from what. You been weldin' longer than that clan you come in with. Knew when I watched you hit a bead the first time. Fine work. Who taught you?"

"My dad."

"Musta been nice learnin' from him."

"Yes. It was," Joel said, staring at Randy's mutilated face.

Randy gently rubbed his cheek. Touched his stitched lip. "Lost my good looks last night. Did the stitchin' myself. Doesn't look pretty."

A man standing on one of the railcars asked, "Yeah, the hell happened? Guys want to know? Ain't nuttin' could be done about it, Randy. C'mon. Tell us."

"Yeah, Randy," said another man. "Spill it."

"Can't see a man taken you down that easy. You kill him?" Fox Redman asked. "Don't be shy."

The whistle blew for lunch, drowning out the men's requests for Randy to tell all.

The men filed into a beaten down house out back of the rail shop. The break house, as it was named, consisted of a cement floor, a circular sink for washing up, and one toilet. Nobody ever used the shower.

They fished out their lunches from the fridge and sat around, digging in. Randy sauntered over to the table and cracked open a soda, then unwrapped his tuna fish sandwich.

"Tell it," Joe Manningly said. "We all got to know."

Joe was American Railcars' lead foreman. He was fifty-ish with dark gray hair and stubble of beard growth that gave the appearance he'd spent more time on the streets than he did working a day job. His bib overalls, ripped and filthy, dangled off him.

Word had it Joe wanted a raise. Letting the owners see him in such tattered attire might, Joel figured, constitute a raise in his wages. Five years from now Joe would be crushed beneath the steel and bolts of a jacked up railcar. Four days later he would die of his injuries. His family would receive half a million dollars from the incident.

"Can't be any worse than what happened to Joe here." Harley Sullivan spouted with a sly grin.

"You just keep that trap shut, Harley," Joe said. "Kick your goddamn ass out in the cold, you don't watch it."

"Tell you what," Harley said. "You tell yours, Randy, and I'll tell Joe's story. Cool?"

Randy grinned. He chewed on his tuna sandwich. "Okay."

"You ever lovin' son-of-a-bitch." Joe jumped up. Ten other men stood quick, ready to toss *Joe* out of the house, and into the cold. Joe was having none of that. He sat back down, grumbling. "Fine," Joe said. "But I'll be tellin' it." He wagged a finger.

"No need." Randy shoved the last bit of his sandwich into his mouth and swallowed. "I'll tell you what happened. No secrets here. Joe don't want to talk about himself, I'll tell ya'll what happened to me. Let's get to it." He unwrapped his second sandwich, took a bite. "I mean having a wife and six kids, then getting held up by a transvestite hooker for nine hundred bucks can be right embarrassing for a man."

Six months ago after work, Joe had picked up a hooker on the strip. This wasn't your nice and tidy strip you might see in Las Vegas. No. The strip consisted of cracked sidewalks with month long growth of weeds seeping up from under the sidewalks; strip clubs for hungry men on payday and on weekends. Well, Joe got himself a real winner and took her out to the rail graveyard; a place known for broken down old Amtrak passenger cars. Wasn't but about a hundred or so feet from American Railcar. A body had once been found crammed beneath one of those cars with six thousand dollars stuffed in his sock.

Joe cashed his check and bounded back and picked up a real honey; tall with legs that went all the way up. A real piece of work, this gal. Smooth ebony skin. Just the way Joe liked them. In Joe's haste, he hadn't noticed the large lump protruding from the hooker's throat, or the size of her hands. Joe got her out there alone and unzipped his fly. When he grabbed that old hooker's hair to push her head down on his cock, it came off in his hands. The hooker brought up the knife to Joe's throat, said he wanted all the money he had. Joe got taken for nine-hundred bucks that afternoon.

"Jesus Christ," Joe said as he threw his Subway across the

room. It hit the wall. Shards of lettuce, onion, ham and tomato sent shrapnel everywhere.

"He did save face, boys," Harley said, looking around the room at the men. "That blow job cost him nine-hundred big ones. But he paid me back every cent. Just so you know. Didn't want his old lady finding out, so I did what any friend would do. I loaned him the nine big ones."

By now the men were busting at the seams.

"You're shitting us," Joel said.

"Nope," Harley said.

"Goddamnit, Harley." Joe slunk back into his seat burying his face in his hands.

"Get on with it, Randy," Pickle said. "Times wastin'. What happened?"

"I got mugged this morning."

The room fell silent.

"Two this morning. We was leavin' the meat packing plant down on Fifth and Willow. You know the place. Been working there part-time three years now, and me and a few guys walked out just past the security fence going to our cars when we got it by four black dudes with pistols. They led us at gun point down a ways out of sight. Thought for sure they was gonna open up on us. One guy about thirty something pissed his jeans good."

"They got us all in an alley alone and held those pistols right in our faces. Then they said to hit our knees. Knew right then and there we was gonna buy the farm. Take what we got and split with the take. So I said to one of them, I said, 'I ain't got much of nothin'. Why you doin' this? Why don't ya'll take off?'"

"Christ all mighty," Harley said. "You said that?"

"Yeah," Randy said biting into his sandwich. "Short and Stocky pistol whipped the shit outta me good and stepped back like he was checking out his handiwork. His buddies thought it was a real hoot. 'I'll ask the questions,' he told me. By now the other guys I'm with start pullin' out their wallets, slipping their rings off. I'm not down for that so I said, 'I give you my wallet, you give it back once you empty it. Don't mind you takin' what I got. But I want that wallet back."

"You're crazy, old coot," one of the men said. "What'd they do then?"

"Short and Stocky got me again. This time it got bad. 'fore he was done blood was all over the place—me, the guy next to me. I think he puked. Not sure. That pistol got my brains scrambled all up. Told me I should keep my cracker mouth shut if I knew what was good for me."

"Hell you care about some old damn wallet, Randy?" Joel asked. "You could've been killed."

"And I've seen that wallet," Pickel said. "Things fallin' apart. Faded all to hell."

"My daddy gave me that wallet," Randy said. "And there ain't no fucker takin' my wallet. So I tell Short and Stocky my daddy gave me the wallet on his deathbed, and that I wanted it back."

Joe no longer buried his face in his hands.

The whistle blew.

Nobody moved.

"Anyway, the next thing I know Short and Stocky is on me fast. I think even his buddies think he's lost it. I mean the guy's on me and swinging that pistol down so hard my lip split wide open and dangled down over my bloody teeth. My face goes all numb like he beat it off. I can't feel anything. He worked on me a good while, then he stood up. When I got my marbles I rose up and saw him buckled over hugging his knees, catching his breath. The pistol was gone. One his buddies held it for him, I guess. I didn't see it. Now the guys I'm with are pissed at me and scared shitless. Told me I say another word, they'll take that gun and shoot me themselves.

"Short and Stocky took my wallet. He opened it. Plucked everything out, tossed away what he didn't want, and jammed the good stuff back inside the wallet. He grinned as he slipped the wallet into his coat pocket. I could tell his buddies weren't the least impressed with him beating down on me the way he did. They left us alive."

"Lucky bastard," Joe said. "You file a report?"

"Did you?" Randy stared at Joe coldly. Joe had nothing, and eased back in his seat again. "The others I was with broke for it. Left me there. Cocksucker took my wallet anyway. Soon as I could I crawled after 'em. Got outta the alley and saw 'em walkin' down the street like nothin' happened. Like it was an every night thing what they was doin' to folks. Short and Stocky saw me crawl out into the street. He just stood there gawking at me like it was the first time he'd seen a white boy. There we were, staring each other down—me lying on the street, him standing tall. He shook his head, pulled out my wallet. I couldn't see what he was doin' cause of my eye was swollen shut by then.

"Short and Stocky held up my wallet, said, 'Want it back? I'll leave it in this here mail box. Aight.' I could see that much," Randy said. "I'd lost a lot of blood by then. Vision kept coming and going. They lit out and I..." Randy pulled out his wallet. Pitched it on the table top. No one touched it. "... crawled my way back to the alley and passed out. Got home round four and stitched my lip and cheek. Head'll be fine, I think. All this," Randy waved a hand in front of his face, "ain't as bad as it looks." He finished his second sandwich and chased it down with an ice cold drink. He looked up at the men. "You know, that ole boy was all right. At least he gave back my wallet."

WHEN DARKNESS FALLS

1

The boy slipped from a hut constructed of branches and deer skin. Under a dark, cloudless night the boy added wood to the dwindling fire, blew on the flames and waved an arm over the encouraging flames, cautious not to burn himself. The forest was quiet.

He followed the footpath down to the brook. He knelt on all fours, cupped icy water into his hands and drank. He did this several times. He listened to the water flow over the rocks. He pinched off a sizable piece of moss from a nearby rock and put it into his mouth. He savored the rich aftertaste of earth and fish as he chewed.

Continuing on, winding his way through the dark without flaw, and skipping over fallen trees he made sure to miss the rough, itchy plants his mother warned him about. Mosquitoes found him and went to work, raising welts all over his body. He made a mental note to apply animal fat to the bites when he returned home, a necessity in the hot seasons.

Up ahead the path forked. He followed the path on the right.

Trees thinned around him, and opened a wider path. Rock and dirt and a single chain of grass rolled down the center. The boy stepped out from amid the trees. He ambled down the path coming to a tall wire fence. Beyond the enclosure sat the house others cautioned him about. A light burned in one window. A sound similar to a million bees gave him pause. He'd known some to touch it and never wake up.

Turning toward home, something lifted him off the ground.

He thought it might be one of them. His insides went cold. The boy let out a feeble yelp. A man stared down at him, eyes cold and infuriated.

"What you doing here?" His father slapped him hard. The boy's teeth clacked together from the blow. The boy struggled, freed himself and drew away. "Answer," said his father. His hair mussed and tangled; veins like steel cords shown under his muscular chest.

"Watching!" said the boy. "I didn't go near. I saw a boy last time. My age."

"They're coming! Not good to be here. You know the law. They come tonight."

The boy's face throbbed from his father's rage, dashed into the forest and away, but his father was faster. He caught up to the boy and slapped him twice more.

"Silence," said his father. "You'll put us all in danger."

Both son and father barreled headlong through the thicket to escape the imminent threat. The boy listened to his father's labored breaths, winced in pain each time his father squeezed his hand.

"Faster," whispered his father. "They kill us sure they find us."

Then a low chanting began. His father threw them both to the ground behind a fallen sap tree. The man covered the boy's mouth with a massive, dirt encrusted hand.

"Say nothing." The father held his son to him. The boy felt the man's heart beat. He'd never seen his father afraid. This frightened him. Home seemed so far away now.

The boy didn't move. He didn't speak.

In the gloom something slammed atop the fallen sap tree. Claws bounded up and down the tree's length.

Clickity—clack—clickity—clack.

The boy feared being crushed alive should the tree roll. The thing grunted atop the tree sniffed the air; clawed at the bark. The boy trembled at the sound.

Then it was gone.

His father allowed a long exhausted breath. He'd been holding it as long as be could. Another second they might've been found. "Stay," he said to the boy. Then he got up. Crouched behind the tree, he studied the area carefully. More were coming, but far in the distance. The man snatched up the boy in his arms and ran for home. A storm was on the horizon.

Inside the hut the boy found the old jar they kept the animal fat in and spread it over his arms, chest, and legs. The itching dissipated some. His mother slept serenely.

The boy handed the bowl to his father. The old man showed no sign of sympathy.

"Sorry," was all the boy could manage. He trembled in his father's presence.

His father doctored his bites and scratches. Then with eyes furious and wild he pulled the boy close. "Stay away from that house!"

The boy nodded, then crawled over to his mother. He placed a hand on her bare thigh, shook her awake. She jumped with a start, then smiled up at her son, brushed a strand of hair out of his eyes. She saw the handprint. The boy need not tell her. She knew.

Her eyes found her husband. She never questioned him. But now seeing her son's swollen face, she did. "What happened?" she asked bitterly.

"He went to the house. We had to hide from *them*. Close tonight."

The woman rose up and scolded the boy. "Never again! Hear? It is a bad place." Her face softened and she kissed the boy's warm, sweaty cheek. She peeled back her deer-skinned blanket, rolled onto her back. "Come," she said as she parted her legs.

The boy mounted her as his father looked on. Their bodies polished with animal fat, he slid his shaft inside of her. The woman's breath caught in her chest; withering beneath him as he moved forward. She lifted her legs, grasped his thighs. She pulled him deeper inside her. They kissed with opened mouths; pawing at one another as her walls constricted. She became louder. The boy held her close. She arched her back, both releasing simultaneously.

They lay together for a long time. His shaft tingled as he slipped out of her. She wiped the sweat off of his face lovingly, and then kissed him with an open mouth; teasing him with her tongue as thunder claps rolled in.

Chad stood in darkness, stared at his grandfather for a long time. He loathed everything about the old man. The way he smelt, the way his long gray hair dropped over cold, dark eyes.

Max lit a corncob pipe. The tobacco smoldered. He shook the match out and threw it into the hearth, rocking in his chair.

Shadows danced on the walls. Chad cringed as his grandfather nibbled at a boil on his arm. Sometimes he spat them out and sometimes he didn't. Chad's stomach knotted.

"Chad," his grandfather said. "Chad, I know you're there. Come out into the firelight so I can see you."

Chad's tongue lay broken; his flesh crawled as he neared his grandfather. Chad closed his eyes, hoping that this was just a dream. Yet he knew better. His father had dropped him off nearly an hour ago and wouldn't be back till morning.

"Come. Sit with me. I want to tell you a story. A story about the year 1922. I think you will enjoy it." The old man cleared his throat, smiled a mouth full of rotten teeth.

Chad hesitantly walked over and sat next to his grandfather. The fire was warm. The goose bumps left and he relaxed. For the most part. He brushed the hair away from his eyes and sat Indian style, cupping his head in his hands.

"Are you ready to take this journey with me? Just you and I?" Chad nodded as his grandfather went on.

"Good. It was 1922 when it all went down. Crazy old bastards, I'll tell you. Hard to believe I still live this close to them. The place where it all happened. Last of the children, I am. The others are gone now, along with our fathers. Oh, I'm not proud of what we did. That's not why I'm telling you this, Chad. It was a time of unrest and violence in these parts. Never told your father about this so let's just keep it between us.

"Don't know why we did it. Some of us kids tried to make ourselves feel better by saying our fathers ordered us to do it. Ordered seems much better. But I can't. Tell the truth, Chad, I enjoyed that day very much. So did the other men. You could see it in their faces, their eyes.

"Times were different. Coal mines kept this town from drying up, so when the strike hit, our fathers thought it'd be a good thing to make the owners give better wages and safer working conditions. That, I'm afraid, wasn't to be. Owners hired scabs to replace my father and the others. Couldn't find brave enough scabs over here to do the job, so they hired them from overseas—Poland, I think." His grandfather inhaled deeply on his corncob pipe. He stared down at Chad with lifeless eyes. He went on.

"It got so bad, at times, we thought we wouldn't be eating. Papa had to go out hunting for food and what not. Got pails of water from the spring to heat on the cook stove. Tell you me, I'll never eat another potato or flapjack again. So the strike continued. Men became restless, started toting guns out to the mines. 'Course, I heard all this from papa when he'd return home end of his shift of walking the line. Me and mama was so scared."

Chad scooted closer to hear every word now.

"Then one day the inevitable happened, Chad. Things got to their boiling point. Gunfire erupted. We lived so close me and mama could hear it—the whole town heard too. It was like church bells it was so loud. Me and mama stepped out on the porch just as papa came up runnin'. I tell you that man was smilin', grandson. Ear to ear he was, and grabbed me off that porch and drug me through the yard. Papa said, 'Gonna make a man outta you today, boy,' he'd said. 'Gonna show you how it's done.' At the time I didn't know what to think. Mama was yellin' for him to stop but he kept on until our house was outta sight and we met up with other men and some their boys. They too was my age. Some them kids was cryin'. Not me though. Somethin' big was happening and I wanted to be part of it.

"Well, Chad, truth be told, that ole strike had ended that mornin'. What followed would be etched in my mind forever— things we'd done to those men. Anyway, strike was over and the scabs came outta those mines scared as shit and worried it'd be the last day they'd see sunlight. Papa and his men wanted

blood. Make them pay for what they'd done. But, as I said, the
strike was over. They called in a flatbed truck and hauled all
them scabs off the property. They wasn't about five miles off
the land when a car come rollin' down the road kicking up so
much dust that when it cut off the flatbed truck, all that dust
swallowed up everything. When it cleared, a man got out, said,
'Kill all you can.' This was what papa told me later."

The old man looked at the dwindling fire. "Chad, if you
don't mind, put another log on the fire, will you?"

"Sure," Chad said. He got up, went to the pile of neatly
stacked logs, and selected one. He tossed it gently into the
flames and went back to sit down. Rain began to fall outside as
the flames rolled around the untouched log. Thunder, once in
the distance, was now directly overhead. The slightest rumble
shook the old house. Chad scooted closer to his grandfather,
forgetting about the smell of him, forgetting his fear. The men
on the flatbed truck had taken all that away now.

2

B ret Lane opened his eyes in total darkness. Weak and bat-
tered, he tried to move his arms, but quickly realized that he
was chained to the wall. His arms and legs were spread apart
as if to make a snow angel. At first he thought he heard voices.
Perhaps that was what woke him. He listened carefully. Yes.
He knew right away that he wasn't alone.

Silence.

He listened hard to hear the voices again. The rumbling of
thunder choked out all other sounds.

*It's hopeless. I'm obviously down in the basement. Is there anyone
else down here with me?*

Silence.

"Is anyone down here?"

Silence.

"Make a noise. Grunt…. Groan."

Silence.

"Is anyone fucking down here with me?"

If he screamed, the man behind the voice might come to

investigate. Better not to scream. His chains appeared bolted to the wall. Even with his strength, he couldn't budge the bolted foundation of the chain. He tried the same with his legs. It was hopeless. He was stuck.

He focused, trying to remember the man from last night. He had pulled off the road, the temp gauge buried in the red when a pair of lights rolled to a stop behind him. At first he thought it was a state trooper coming to investigate the problem. The driver got out and walked up to his Mustang.

Bret looked over his shoulder to see a shadow pass the window and spun around. A large figure outside the window waited for him to wind down the window.

"You all right, son?"

"Car overheated on me," Bret said. "Just took its last breath, I believe."

"Be glad to give you a lift into town. No sense walking that far. Besides, storm's on the way. You'll never make it into Springfield before it hits."

Bret collected his smokes on the dash, grabbed his leather jacket from the passenger seat.

He got into the pickup truck and relaxed for the forty-mile ride to Springfield. The driver got in and started the truck. Bret drew a cigarette from the pack. "Mind if I smoke?"

"Not at all," the old man said. "I smoked thirty years before I finally kicked the habit. Don't mind at all."

Bret lit the cigarette and inhaled soothingly. He noticed the truck was a sixties model with the stick shift on the side. The thing sounded like a tank wheeling down the road. A stack of discolored newspapers lay on the dash. A collection of empty beer cans flooded the floorboard.

"Do much drinking?" Bret asked. He scooted them about, freeing his feet. A light mist hit the windshield as the storm closed the gap quickly. The old man smiled and nodded. Bret rolled the window down and flicked the cigarette out the window.

The old man took a cup off the dash and pointed to a thermos on the seat between them. "Have some coffee. It'll warm the soul a bit."

Bret poured himself a glass. "Thanks."

"Don't mention it. Glad I still had some left."

Bret gulped the contents quickly and poured another cup. Before he could drink the second cup his vision grew blurry. His body felt numb all over and shortly thereafter he remembered falling into darkness.

And now, chained to the wall, he tasted blood in his mouth.

3

Chad sat spellbound, his eyes locked on his grandfather. "Go on," Chad said. "Finish the story. Did you kill them?"

"Kill them?" his grandfather laughed. "What we done should've never been allowed to happen. I think that now. Some part of me regrets it. But, as I said, times were different. Survival, Chad. And no, I don't full heartedly regret it. I enjoyed most of what we did."

The old man took a long drag from the pipe and frowned. "When we got to town some them scabs were still alive and on the run. Papa and the other men killed a lot of them up at the cemetery. Some were found tangled in barbed wire where they tried to climb over and failed. But the ones in town, as my papa told us boys, was ours for the killin'.

"My father and his men opened up with their rifles and shotguns. Not to kill, mind you, but to wound. Let's see." The old man looked far off in thought. "There was Danny Cummings, me, Billy Greer, Thomas O'Neal, and Patrick Hughes. Rest of the boys took to runnin' off. For us it was magic time. Our fathers handed us knives and told us to go to work. We did."

"No one stopped it?" Chad asked.

"Too afraid to," the old man said. "Guess they thought they'd get it too if they interfered. Me and the boys went to cutting the throats of the living and dying that day. Right there on Main Street under God and the whole damn town of Herrin. Not a hand was raised to stop us. No one dared. Not with my father and the rest looking on. Nothin' like pulling back the head of a man and letting a blade sink into soft flesh, dear boy. Nothing like it at all. Them scabs was cryin' and begging for their lives right down to the last man. I'd drop a knee on their back, snatch a lock of hair, pull back, and let the knife do the rest. Easy as sayin' your prayers at night.

"Got so it was like riding a bike. Sometimes I'd work on their faces before ending them. Papa liked that. Said I had imagination. After it was done, we stacked the bodies in Nathan Broil's General Store. Nathan was none too thrilled with the idea, but he didn't protest right off. Truth be told, town folk was happy and ready to get back to work. The law finally made us cart the bodies off. We buried them in a mass grave up here on the mountain. Not too sure where it's at now, but close. Wasn't too much later we heard a few scabs and their families hightailed it up into the mountains. We searched for weeks. Never found them. Not a trace. Some have said they live wild up here. Mixing up with the animals and such. Said some are as normal as me and you. Others say the ones we killed come back from the grave as something else. Beasts, they said. Truth be told, they all probably died of starvation or sickness." The old man pointed at the window. "Right out there somewhere.

"Mama didn't speak much after that. She went all inward on us. Wasn't two years later she caught the coughing sickness and died. Daddy went ten years later when a wall collapsed in on him and several other men in the mines. Strange thing was, it was the same men who did the killin'. Bizarre. Guess there is justice after all. Then the boys I was with that day started dropping off when they got older. It was as if them scabs had put a curse on all of us.

"Built this house after I married your grandmother. Oh, how she loved this place. Peaceful, it was. We had your daddy, we lived soon good lives. I forgot about those men in 1922 for the most part. Got on with my life. Then one day your grandma went out to pick strawberries and never come back. I got some men in town and we searched all over this mountaintop. It was as if the mountain had swallowed her up like them scabs in 1922. People now and again go missing up here."

"That why you put up the fence, Grandpa?" asked Chad.

The old man smiled grimly, looked at his watch. "Time for you to get to bed. That's for another story, boy."

"One more, Grandfather. Please. One more story."

"Not tonight. Next time you spend the night." The old man stood and walked Chad to the spare bedroom. "I'll wake you in the morning."

Chad got into bed and pulled the covers around him tightly. "You won't change your mind?"

"I'm sure. Grandpa's going to be busy tonight."

"I saw a boy today," Chad said. "He was standing outside the fence, along the side."

"Trick of the morning light, maybe," his grandfather said. "Ain't no kids up on this here mountain."

"But I saw him. My age, he was."

His grandfather chuckled. "This mountain plays tricks, son," His grandpa said. "Now, off to sleep with you." Chad grumbled, closed his eyes and rolled over.

He slept.

Max went to the closet and retrieved his rifle.

He loaded it, walked outside.

The twelve-foot chain-link fence surrounding his property gave him a sweet feeling of comfort. Moonlight bathed the house and the crest of the forest.

He looked at his watch.

Ten-thirty.

The rain, coming down harder now, made it difficult to see.

He remembered the first time he saw them. That was prior to electrifying the fence for protection, before they realized he existed here. It opened a door of opportunity for him to learn about them, to study their hunting skill. They never hunted alone, always together in a pack. They reminded him of wolves; however, these creatures were much more evolved. Smartest damn things Max had ever seen. They were almost human.

One would expose itself to its prey while the others moved in. It had been that way with the deer a few years back. Max had watched the deer just after dark on the gravel drive just outside the fence. Unaware of him, it grazed.

One of the little bastards popped out of the shadows taking care not to make a sound. Instinctively, the deer bolted away.

The creatures leapt swiftly and took the buck down without a struggle. After making quick work of their kill, they vanished into the forest.

Now, remembering the way they had torn that deer to ribbons, Max went back inside to prepare for their arrival as always.

The moon would be full tonight.

They'll be coming soon, he thought.

4

Bret lifted his head when he heard what sounded like a door unlocking. He struggled with the chains, but it was no use. He also tried sliding his hands through the cuffs. It was pointless.

Silence.

The upstairs door opened suddenly. The dark basement glowed with a dim light from upstairs. Firelight perhaps. He stared around the room catching glimpses of other dangling chains. He saw their long dark shapes bolted to the wall.

Letting his eyes wander, he found a table off to the left. It appeared to be an operating table. Terrified, Bret jerked quickly on the chain. The cuffs tightened when he did this. He let out a small yelp.

Footsteps now.

"I'm not the first," Bret said to himself. He saw the other chains. He saw the bloodstained wall. He saw everything.

He listened.

"I can hear you," Max said. "It would have done you no good to scream. I built this basement just as I built this house."

The basement door slammed shut.

Click.

Bret's throat went dry.

"What are you going to do to me?" Bret asked. The dim light was gone now.

Darkness.

Silence.

Bret heard the man coming down the steps, the ring of keys clanking together as he descended. A fluorescent light blinked to life over the table to the left of him.

Bret had barely been able to see the man in the truck, but now standing face to face with him he realized the man was much larger than he had anticipated. The old man walked with a limp, his hair hiding his face most of the time as he made his way to the table.

"I want to thank you for coming tonight," he said. "I hope you'll understand what is about to happen. There will be no hard feelings, at least with me."

"Hard feelings?" Bret said. "You kidnapped me."

"Not really," added the old man. "You willingly got in my truck. There was no refusal from you."

Stuffed neatly between the back of his pants and shirt, Max slid his hunting knife out and showed it to Bret.

"If you move, my friend here is going to cut you," Max explained. "Do you understand?"

Bret didn't move.

Max unbuckled Bret's belt and unzipped his pants. After doing that he bowed and cut the pants cuffs to the knees and removed Bret's shoes.

"What are you doing?" Bret asked. "Let me go, please. I won't say anything to anyone. I give you my word."

"I know you won't. And I promise I will let you go," Max said. "I give you my word. Just as soon as I'm done with you."

Max removed Bret's belt and did the same with his pants, slicing each side to the knee. Bret began to sob.

"Fucking baby," Max scoffed. Next, with a downward stroke, he slashed the underpants as well.

Bret flinched.

"I TOLD YOU NOT TO MOVE!" Max shouted. He brought the knife to Bret's chest and gently poked him.

Bret screamed.

Immediately, the blade moved down, slicing through flesh and muscle.

Bret screamed louder.

Max paused, the blade still deep within Bret's chest. When Bret stopped screaming Max asked, "Didn't I tell you not to move?"

Bret nodded.

With a swift downward stroke, Max cut through the left nipple, and watched it fall to the floor.

Bret screamed louder than ever.

Max snatched his balls and tightened quickly. Bret's face went pale.

"NO-NO-NO!"

"Are you going to be nice?"

"Y-yes."

When Max was sure of this he loosened his grip around Bret's testicles and finished cutting off his shirt.

"You're going to kill me, aren't you?" Bret said.

"I told you I would let you go. Are you calling me a liar?" Bret shook his head, frightened. "No. Of course not."

He looked down at his bleeding chest. The wound was deep, his left nipple gone.

He began to cry.

Max went to the cabinet and removed two smaller sets of chains. He returned to Bret and attached the chains to his wrists and ankles. With the keys, he removed the first set chaining him to the wall.

"Just so we're clear, you're not free," Max said. "This is to keep you silent while we leave the basement. Don't need you running through my home, do we?"

"You're really letting me go?"

"Of course I am. I told you I'm a man of my word." Max guided Bret to the other side of the basement. "Now if you try and run before I get the chains off or attack me while I'm unlocking you, I'll split you like a grapefruit. Do we understand each other?"

Bret nodded.

"Good."

The old man grabbed him by the elbow. Bret stopped. The old man reached for the knife.

"No," Bret quickly reacted. "I just wanted to know where we were going that's all."

Max released his grip on the knife. "Outside," he said. "I'm taking you to the front gate. Then I'll release you."

They started walking again, taking careful steps up the stairs.

Max dug into his pants pocket and brought the keys into the light. He fumbled through them quickly and selected one.

"I gave you my word that I wouldn't tell a soul," Bret said. "I mean that. I really do."

Max chuckled. "I trust you won't. That's why I'm letting you go. Sorry for the cut. But I told you not to move," Max explained. "When you're told to stay still, you do it. I was just having fun." Max inserted the key and unlocked the door. He opened it and glanced around before continuing with his prisoner. When all was safe he tugged on Bret to follow.

The front room had the scent of mold and wet leaves. The room, apparently the living room, was cozy. The firelight burned his eyes. He tried to shelter them with his hand, but the old man squeezed tightly on his elbow when he tried it. He was so busy glancing around the room he hadn't noticed the old man pick up the rifle.

Max stopped, snatched a remote control off the shelf above the fireplace and pushed it into the breast pocket of his shirt. He opened the front door and stepped out onto the porch holding tight to Bret.

Max heard the electrical fence singing. He always remembered to turn it on before dark. He wasn't that absentminded yet. If he forgot to turn the fence on it would be the death of….

Suddenly a bolt of lightning streaked across the sky. Sparks flew on the right side of the house.

Silence.

Nearly to the front gate, Max turned Bret loose and headed for the house shouting, "The generator, I've got to start it!" Nearly tripping up the steps, Max regained his balance and vanished inside the house.

Bret bolted toward the fence, then remembered seeing a rifle in the old man's hand and stopped cold. Max would pick him off before he got to cover, especially with his legs and ankles chained.

Something climbed the fence to the left of him. Bret hobbled toward the porch. He tried gaining speed, but was afraid he would most certainly fall. He paused at the first step and realized he had to hop one at a time.

By this time, two of them were over the fence.

Bret hopped the second step nearly losing his balance and falling over.

Now there were four.

He watched their shapes coming at him, low to the ground at a gallop.

Two steps left. He leaped hard this time, cleared both and skipped toward the door.

They were coming up the steps now. Behind him he could feel their breath, their claws clicking on the boards. He stumbled inside and threw the door shut, locking the dead bolt as one crashed into the door. He let himself drop to the floor, trying to catch his breath. He felt like vomiting, but didn't.

At first, Bret was sure the man was going to shoot him as soon as he left the gate. Why else would he have brought the rifle? Then it hit him.

He was going to feed me to them.

Beads of sweat rolled down his chest and arms. The radiant firelight seemed to choke him now as he sat alone, the steady howls from the creatures growing ever louder. The doorknob began to turn.

5

Max picked up the rifle as he realized something important. Chad! He left the useless generator behind and broke for his grandson's room.

How could he have forgotten his own flesh and blood?

Chad snapped out of sleep to find his grandfather shaking him wildly. "Huh…. What?"

He rubbed his eyes, yawning.

"Chad, wake up," Max ordered.

"What is it?" Chad mumbled.

"Chad, Grandpa needs you to do something. I need you to get under the bed. Can you do that for me?"

Chad, half asleep, nodded.

"Hurry, boy,"

"Is everything all right?" Chad asked.

Glass shattered somewhere in the house.

"Everything's fine, son. Just get under the bed and don't come out. Do you understand? Whatever you hear coming from the house, under no circumstances are you to come out!"

Chad agreed, and climbed out of bed. He watched from beneath the bed as his grandfather vanished from sight.

Max returned to the living room to find Bret sitting on the floor, back against the door, and weeping into his hands. For a moment, Max felt pity for the guy. After all, it wasn't his fault that this happened. He had no one to blame but himself. He fished out the keys and threw them at the man's feet.

"Unlock yourself," he told him. "There's one thing I love in all this fucked up world, and that's my grandson. If'en you help me, I'll let you go."

"Like you were going to let me go just now?" Bret said, his face still buried in his hands. "Your grandson can burn in hell with you, as far as I'm concerned."

Enraged, Max ran at Bret and picked him off the floor. He raised the rifle at point blank range, but not before slapping him around a few times. "You've got two seconds to live, you son of a bitch! If you don't help me, I'll take you out right here!"

Bret threw his hands up in front of the barrel, backing up against the door.

"All right," Bret snapped. "I'll help. Just don't shoot me."

Bret removed the handcuffs, stepped away from the door, and went to the window next to the fireplace.

"My God."

"How many?" asked Max.

"I don't know. It's raining too hard. They're moving too fast. Did you hear the glass shatter?"

"Sounded like it came from upstairs," Max said, vanishing down the corridor. When he returned he had pants, socks, and a shirt. He threw them to Bret. "Put 'em on. You're gonna need them to fight the fuckers."

"Fight?"

"You don't wanna fight with your cock hanging out, do you?"

Bret shook his head.

Max went to the stack of wood and selected a log for the fire as the room grew dark. He threw it in and grabbed the poker. "Can't let the fire go out now. They'll be coming down the chimney."

Crack!

Something large struck the side of the house.

Crack!

Glass shattered.

"What about the basement? Can we hold them off down there?"

Bret really didn't want to go back down there, but if it was the only way to survive the creatures then he would. He found himself going back to the window and looking out into the yard.

A fist hammered the door.

Both men twirled around nearly falling. Max aimed the rifle.

6

Frightened, Chad slid out from under the bed, and ran to the doorway. Fearful of disobeying his grandfather, he had just about decided to go back to his hiding place, when a voice called out his name in the darkness.

"Chad."

It wasn't coming from the living room, but to the left of him, further down the corridor. Chad looked to the voice, but couldn't see anyone.

"Hurry, this way. Come down here."

The voice was raspy and deep. Almost like an animal. Chad ran toward the darkness. He thought his grandfather might've been hurt, but quickly realized that wasn't so when something stepped into the corridor directly in front of him, and snatched him up.

7

"You just try and I'll splatter your fucking brains!" Max shouted at the door.

"You can't kill us all, old man," a deep raspy voice said. "It'll be so much easier if you don't fight us. Now open the door. You're the last one."

Silence.

Max, still aiming the rifle at the door, approached it slowly.

"Have you gone insane?" Bret blurted. "They'll kill both of us, not to mention your sweet grandson."

Max stopped and lowered the rifle. "You're right. Even if I shoot the one at the door, the others will rush us."

"Can I ask you something?" asked Bret. He tucked his shirt in and stepped toward the man.

Max stepped away from the door, the rifle still tight in his grasp. "Ask away."

"Tell me the truth. What was your plan for me and what are those creatures?"

"The plan was to feed you to the bastards outside," Max said. "I had no intention of releasing you. The rifle was for my protection."

"So I was right."

Max nodded.

"I've been feeding those damn things a long time now. At first there were only a few that I knew of. Then they began to multiply."

Bret found a seat on the floor next to the fireplace and ran his fingers through his hair. "They know you. It spoke your name. Why?"

Max was just as alarmed as Bret when the thing spoke. As a matter of fact, he was scared to answer any more questions, yet he knew the man had more.

"I've brought men to this house," Max said. "Feed 'em to keep those bastards at bay." He told him the story of the mineworkers and the strike so many years ago. "I'm the last."

"I've heard the stories."

"Knew one day they'd catch up to me. That's why I put up the fence. There are others out there who escaped that fateful day, but they bother nothing. Keep to themselves mostly. But those," he pointed to the door. "Those are the ones we helped kill and finish off.

"Do you know what it's like to hear a man scream for his life? The power you feel is beyond anything in the world." He trailed off suddenly, listening to the storm. "Like you, I took them to the gate and promised them release."

"They believed you?"

"Of course they believed me," Max said. "Some made it pretty far I expect. Others didn't get out of sight before those things hit. You should have seen them screaming and clawing at the earth, trying to get away. Pleading with me to open the gate."

"And you just stood there watching?"

After that both men sat in silence. Eventually, Max drew out a pouch of tobacco. He filled his pipe and was about to light it when a shadow emerged from the darkness of the corridor unseen.

8

"What'll we do with him?" a voice asked.

Chad sat on the lawn, rain pelting his flesh, hair matted to his scalp. Shaking, Chad curled his knees to his face. He was sobbing, his cheeks mixed with rain and tears. His pajamas were torn at the knee. His elbow was scraped from the broken glass.

"He is just a boy," one of the creatures said. "He's not to be harmed."

"Then why did you eat of my flesh?"

"That was different," the larger creature said.

The smaller of the two stepped forward clenching the other's arm. "You murdered me. You and the others hunted me down and ate my flesh." The creature pulled the other closer. "You passed on your curse to others. What is the difference if we kill the boy?"

"Because I was the first," the larger one said, and slashed out. The smaller creature released his grip and moved away. "I've watched this old house for years. We were reincarnated somehow. With only me, I knew I couldn't kill the man. But as time went on, after each prey, our numbers began to grow. It stops tonight. This child is innocent. The young one cannot be harmed. If he is, you'll answer to me, and the others who suffered alongside me that day so long ago."

They all appeared to be animals, yet spoke human. Chad was glad the bigger creature protected him. If he hadn't been here, it's possible they would have attacked. The creatures began to spread out now, away from the boy, and the creature that protected him. When it was just the two of them, the creature heard the boy speak.

"Where do you come from?" Chad asked.

The larger creature looked down at him. He grunted and shuffled forward. "Why do you ask?"

Chad shrugged.

For a moment the creature appeared to be humored. "We come from the earth. Down below. Don't ask me how I got here." The beast moved closer.

Chad gasped.

"Don't be afraid. I'll not hurt you. Nor will the others." He glanced at the two laying near the house. "If they try they'll end up like them."

"I'm...."

"I know who you are. Chad, right?"

Chad nodded.

The creature stuck out his clawed hand in good faith.

Chad recoiled.

"Don't be afraid, Chad. I won't bite."

Chad took the creature's hand.

"That's better. I'm Bobby. Now we know one another." The creature took back his hand.

"You were once like me?"

"Sure was," the creature said. "Just like you. In fact, I knew your grandfather a long time ago."

"Were you one of the men who my grandpa killed in the

story?" Chad asked. "My grandfather told me about it. How he killed people called scabs," Chad explained.

"Did he now?"

"Yeah, and he said the guy was wearing all black and carried a knife. Grandfather said the he stabbed a lot of men that day."

The creature roared and knelt closer to the boy.

Chad began to sob. New tears began to trickle down his face. Trembling, he said, "T-that's j-just what he t-told me."

The creature stepped away from Chad and looked to the house. "Stay here. Don't follow."

9

Bret prepared to stand when something grasped his ankle. Before Bret could scream a warning, he was dragged into darkness. Max leapt to his feet and fired the rifle blindly into the dark. Screams erupted in the house. He knew right away he hadn't shot Bret. He aimed too high, hoping to scare the creature away. It did no such thing. Bret's bloodcurdling screams froze Max's heart.

After being rolled on his back, Bret stared into the yellow eyes of the creature. Black pupils, sharpened teeth, long curved claws.

Another shot exploded, the bullet zipping past his head. The creature stumbled backward, nearly collapsing to the floor. It regained its balance and charged. Bret closed his eyes, screaming.

Max fired a third shot, this time striking the creature's chest. It staggered backward, this time making no advance. Max watched its shadow in the corridor before it fell to the floor.

Bret opened his eyes to find the beast on its side next to him.

He found his way to his feet and made his way to Max, who was still aiming the rifle, his finger on the trigger, the butt firmly placed against his shoulder.

"Thank you." Bret said. "That thing would've killed me."

"Damn right it would have. Me too if I hadn't gotten that lucky shot."

Bret nodded, and passed the old man, patting his shoulder.

"Chad," Max whispered into the darkness. "Chad, come on. It's dead."

Silence.

"Come on, son. It'll be safer for you in here."

More silence.

Walking down the corridor, Max zigzagged from one side to the other, the rifle aimed, finger on the trigger. He slowly made his way to Chad's room. He glanced behind him. Bret had vanished into the living room. He swallowed, the pain made him wince. It felt as though he had quenched his thirst with broken glass.

Barrel first, Max entered the room. "Chad!" he whispered firmly. "Chad, get your ass out from under there, now."

He heard Chad shift under the bed.

"That's it. Come on out."

Under the bed, cloaked in darkness, a pair of yellow eyes waited for the old man to approach.

Hearing the gunshots, Chad stood quickly. Prior to the shots, Chad watched the creatures disappear into the house from a shattered window. Two remained on the roof.

Chad decided against running and sat back down. He didn't want to anger the two on the roof. For all he knew, they were just waiting for him to run. They reminded Chad of the old gargoyles atop the old clock tower in town.

10

Bret was peering out the window when something caught his eye. He rubbed a hand across the windowpane for a clearer view. It was too dark, but he saw one of them sitting in the yard. This one nearly looked human. He squinted, rubbed the window glass again. "Holy shit," he said with alarm. It *was* human, a small child. Bret knocked on the window trying to get the boy's attention.

Max loosened his grip and let the rifle hang to his side as he neared the bed. Behind him, dark shapes eluded him, unaware that they were heading to the living room.

"That's it, son," Max coaxed the frightened boy. On his

hands and knees now, Max turned loose of the rifle and reached out blindly, feeling his way. When his hand vanished under the bed, something took it, something that wasn't his grandson. Max fumbled furiously for the rifle when he felt the bones in his left hand snap.

He screamed.

Bret turned toward the screams and was running down the corridor when he took a blow to the chest. He toppled over a few times before stopping shy of the fireplace.

The creatures walked into the firelight. One of them spoke. "I want the old man alive. This one."

The largest of the creatures came forth. "This one will join us." He looked into Bret's eyes. Before Bret could reply, the creature left the circle. The house full of them now, he heard the voice in the distance.

"Kill 'em!"

Max, holding his broken hand, sat against the wall. He gazed at the rifle. It was worthless now. The barrel was bent and shells were scattered about the floor. "Finish it. Finish what you came here to do," Max said at the beast standing before him. "What's wrong, you fuck! Finish me!"

"In due time," another creature spoke as it entered the room.

Max could hear Bret. No words, just agonizing screams. Sounds of death, sounds of feasting he had heard many times before. Meat ripped away from bone. The smacking sounds made when feeding on their prey.

Then there was silence.

"Nothing to it," the creature said. "You'll wish it was you before we're finished with you. His death was quick. Painful but quick. Yours on the other hand..." The creature clasped its hands together. "Your death will be a legend to remember."

"I've always fed you, all of you. Let me go. Don't kill my grandson! He knows nothing about me. He doesn't know anything about anything."

The creature said nothing.

"Stand him up."

Max began to cry.

"You help them kill us." The creature put a claw to Max's

throat. "Everyone here tonight is because of you. They will all get their turn."

"Remember me?" the other asked. "You hurt me. You wanted to touch, to stick, and to watch me bleed. You laughed when I screamed."

"I'm sorry."

"We know you will be." The creature removed his claw away from Max's throat and motioned for the other to take him. "Get the other one and go to the basement. Chain him to the wall. It's not to start until I return. I have to do something."

The creature led Max down the corridor into the living room, repeating the commands. They filed into the basement.

11

Chad, still sitting, watched as the two creatures climbed down and vanished into the house. Bobby crawled from the window and came to him slowly.

Chad stood.

Bobby placed his clawed hand on his shoulder and said. "It's time for you to leave, Chad. You're free to go."

"My grandfather?"

"I'm afraid he'll be staying with us." He walked Chad to the gate and ripped the padlock from its place. He swung the gates open. He looked down at Chad.

"You're free. On your way now."

"My dad'll be coming to pick me up tomorrow." Chad said. "If I'm not here, he'll lose it."

"You have to go, Chad. You can't stay here. I promise not to hurt your father. I'll leave something for him to find you. Now go to town."

Still afraid, Chad passed the gate.

"Oh, Chad," Bobby said.

"Yes?"

"Never come back here. Ever. Stay away. This place is unholy."

Chad started walking toward the highway.

Halfway there something shifted in the woods. The boy

he'd seen this morning stepped out from behind the trees. Two more figures, eaten by the darkening depths of the forest stood motionless.

Chad waved in greeting. The small boy returned the gesture. The man and woman did not.

Chad kept walking.

BROTHERS

Beth looked over the neighborhood. Dry, dead leaves bordered the street.

The house across the street stood as it always had with its weather-beaten walls and splintering porch. Amid ragweed and crabgrass, a festering, discolored chain-link fence shielded it from the outside world. Beth's eagerness to visit the boy waned as she looked on.

"Boy didn't kill anyone," her mother said. "He didn't have it in him then, doesn't have it in him now."

Beth glared across the street. Didn't matter what her mother said. Her daughter was dead. Found raped, beaten, and murdered at the grain mill. She'd overheard them say river rats found her first. *Took a whole clip to get them off her,* an officer said. Conversations overheard at the station the first day nearly sent her spinning out of control. When they'd seen her they clammed up tight. But she'd heard every word.

Beth turned to her mother. "What if I found proof? Suppose I make him talk. Make him tell me the truth? Scare him."

Her mother sighed, folded her newspaper in her lap. "Honey, we've gone over this. You need to cope with this. I loved her too, Beth. Going after Jacob will solve nothing. He didn't do it." She leaned forward in her chair. "Not a day goes by I don't think about my granddaughter. Times she stayed the night. Times she helped her poor ole grandma in the garden. She loved it, you know, helping in the garden. I remember how she lived, not how she died."

"How do you do it?" Beth asked. "Live with it?"

"I cope," said her mother. "I...fill myself with memories.

Just like I do with your father. I think about the good times."

"I can't."

"You can," her mother said. "I still cry, Beth. If I don't catch myself, sometimes I cry. Late at night. When the house is quiet. Then the good memories I hold so close come back. Remember the time your father forgot to fill the tank in that old puky green Ford pickup truck of his?"

Tears welled up in Beth's eyes. "I remember."

"And how he didn't want to go back to town to fill it, so Sahara went on out there and filled the blasted thing up with water from the garden hose. I thought your father was gonna have a high-speed come apart. But then he stopped and laughed so hard I thought he might fall over deader than a possum. We both laughed. See," her mother said. "Those are the memories I'm talking about. The ones that keep me going. Jesus, haven't thought about that in ages."

Beth moved in with her mother three months after the police found Sahara out at the old grain mill. Beth's husband couldn't manage the fact that somehow, in some small way, Beth was responsible for Sahara's death. Not keeping a better eye on her. Letting her stay out longer—later. Her own breakdown and obsession with Jacob. He didn't believe it any more than her mother. No amount of persuading would budge him. So she'd moved out. She felt in her bones she could keep a better eye on Jacob here. Close but distant.

"I know Jacob did it. Everybody thinks he's perfect but I *know* he's guilty." Beth collected their dishes. "More coffee?"

"A little," her mother said. "And don't put that fake sugar in there. Hate that."

A moment later Beth returned with the coffee. Instead of sitting she stood, stared at the house across the street.

"*...Rats all over her...*"

"*...Eating their way inside to find the good stuff...*"

"*...Must've been thirty of 'em....*"

"*...Found a broken bottle jammed up inside her...*"

Her mother blew gently across the lip of her cup. Steam coiled aloft, fogged her spectacles. "Kid ain't had a life since you accused him. Lost friends, he did. Drgged him through the mud. We've known that boy all our lives. Boy ain't got nothin' no more." She finished her coffee. She stood up. "Think about what I said, honey."

"Nap time?"

"...*Face down in corn mill...*"

"...*No clothes on. Not a stitch...*"

"Yep. Inside for a nap," her mother said. "Keeps these old bones workin'." She turned to Beth before going into the house. "I miss her too, Beth. Loved her just like you. But Jacob ain't no killer. And his brother comes home from college today. Please. Leave it be?"

Beth watched her mother go inside. Her gaze locked on the house across the street. Minutes later she heard the old woman's snoring from the living room sofa. Beth stood. Her hand rested possessively over the pocket of her blouse. Her mother kept a small—a.25—beneath her mattress for protection. Beth had collected the weapon when she went inside.

Jacob looked out the window into the garden. He closed his eyes, relishing the images dancing in his head. He sipped his iced tea.

"I know what you did to Sahara," Beth said. "I know it was you. You're the one who killed my little girl."

"...*face was unrecognizable...*"

"...*big as poodles, they were...*"

Jacob jumped and looked up, startled, to see her standing over him. She had come through the back door, and the thought gave him a chill. She had tears in her eyes. Jacob, at only eighteen, was tall and firmly built, with blond bangs dangling over blue, bitter eyes. He noticed the woman's hand inside the pocket of her blouse.

"I know it was you. You're going to tell me everything. Did you think I'd just let it go?" Beth stepped forward. "Either way I'm ending this today. Going to pump these shells in your chest if you don't come with me."

"...*she's missing all her upper teeth.*"

"I didn't kill her. I swear it." Even he didn't believe the words spilling from his lips.

"Soon as Kirk comes home he'll know his brother's a murderer."

"...*Even took her eyes. Who'd do such a thing...?*"

"...*Nothing we can do, Beth. Jacob's no longer a person of interest...*"

Beth brought out the small handgun. "C'mon, Jacob," she said, holding the gun with a trembling hand. "I know you're not going, so it'll be quicker just the same we go into the backyard. Quicker than what you gave her."

The driver smelt of cigarettes and beer and sweat. He glanced in his rearview mirror, gray eyes pouring over the young man in the back seat.

"Glad to have you home, Kirk. Tell your old man I said hello, will you?" said the cabby. "And tell him to get his ass down to Ely's Place. Gotta win my money back."

"Thanks, Mr. Crawford, I sure will. Pop always did have a soft spot for cards."

"Soft spot, my ass," replied Crawford with a chuckle. "He took me for two hundred bucks."

They veered to the curb and the young man said his painstakingly polite thank yous and goodbyes, paid the fare and pulled his luggage out after him.

Kirk stood on the sidewalk long after the cab had pulled away.

Much had changed in four years. Scarcely visible below stalks of weeds, Kirk followed the cracked, concrete sidewalk to the veranda of the house. Finding the door unlocked, he stepped inside.

Instantly, warm, dank air assaulted his nostrils—something else, too, but he couldn't put a finger on it. Dust blanketed the furnishings. Kirk made his way through the house and into his old bedroom. He found it just as he'd left it.

Never much of a hip-hop fan, Kirk enjoyed the older, hard-rocking bands, such as Dio, Black Sabbath and AC/DC. Posters adorned the walls, along with signed photos of different band members. He wondered how much he'd get for them on eBay.

"Jacob," called Kirk. "You home?"

"Down here," a voice drifted through the house. "In the cellar."

Kirk descended the stairs, navigated around boxes stuffed with assorted junk— Christmas lights, books, and childhood toys. Under a single bare bulb, he froze. An unclothed woman lay at his brother's feet.

"Fuck me..."

Jacob stood over the body.

"I didn't mean to." Spittle dribbled down his chin. "I tried to stop, but I couldn't. I tried. Really."

"You didn't try hard enough." Kirk stumbled forward on weak legs. "What the hell have you done?"

How many girls had Kirk helped bury to conceal his brother's passion? He assumed Jacob's fixation would have ended with him leaving for college, but apparently, it hadn't.

Kirk's legs buckled. He thought for a moment that he was going to vomit. He stared at the body and said, "What have you done?"

"She *knew*, Kirk. She knew everything. She tried to kill me." He tossed the gun to the floor, crossed the room, picked up his pants, pulling them on. "She came over with the gun, said she was going to shoot me. If the gun had been loaded it would've been me laid out."

Kirk sat down on his haunches. "Sick fuck. This woman did nothing to deserve this. If anything," Kirk said as tears welled up in his eyes, "you had it coming. That gun went click, you should've called the cops and got her on home invasion or attempted murder. Something."

"I panicked," Jacob said. "I didn't know what to do."

"Like Sahara?"

"That's not fair."

Kirk remembered Jacob shaking him awake in the middle of the night. He said Sahara had rejected his offers one too many times so he cut her. Jacob had giggled. They'd both taken her out to the grain mill. Kirk wanted out fast but Jacob wasn't finished. "I want to stay a while. You know, hide the body. I'll catch up."

"We knew this woman all our lives. Apple pies in the summer for all the neighborhood kids. Hell, she bought a pool so none of us had to be driven all the way across town to the public one. All us kids loved her—even you. This won't go away.

They'll hunt for her until they find her. Old woman across the street fought for you when no one else would. Now you've taken her daughter, and her granddaughter." Kirk was quiet for a long time. Then he said: "How long until dad gets home?"

"About five hours."

"Go out to the shed and get the tarp. Then come back down here."

"What are we gonna do?"

"Get the tarp."

Jacob did.

Kirk busied himself upstairs in the kitchen. He pulled out a large pot. He began with tomatoes, onions, peppers and potatoes, and hamburger. He cut them up, pitched the concoction into the pot, then walked down to the basement and waited for Jacob.

In the basement, they rolled the woman onto the tarp.

"Here," Kirk said, giving a knife to Jacob. "I'll start down here with the legs."

"What are we gonna do?"

"Take her out back and bury her," Kirk said. "We'll bury her all around the backyard."

They went to work.

When it was done, the basement smelt of a meatpacking plant. They carted the woman out back, rolled up in their father's tarp. Kirk got the shovel and started digging.

Kirk said, "I dig. You plant."

"Okay."

Four and a half hours later, Kirk stood under the shower for what seemed an eternity, while his brother torched their clothes and tarp outside in the burn barrel.

Kirk turned off the water and toweled off. He looked in the mirror. His skin was rubbed raw from the hot water and the scrubbing. Satisfied he had not missed anything, he dressed and stepped out into the hallway.

He found the pot of stew steaming on the table. It smelled wonderful. He stirred the contents carefully.

"You handled this well."

"Thank you," said Kirk. "Everything's cleaned up, right?"

"Far as I know," Jacob said. " Ole girl across the street was easy. Found her sleeping on the couch. Little pillow therapy."

"Jesus!"

"What?"

"Someone could've seen you," Kirk said. "Idiot."

"I took the alley. Back door was unlocked."

The screen door opened and slammed shut.

Kirk and Jacob took their seats at the table. They could hear water running in the bathroom.

"Something smells delicious," said a stern, deep voice from the bathroom. The man, bearded and burly, shuffled into the room moments later, face half washed.

"There's my boy." Their father grabbed Kirk up in a bear hug. "Glad to see you home, son. Been too long."

"Sure has," Jacob said. "Even if it is for a short time."

Their father filled his bowl, looked up at the boys. A kind of sadness fell over him. For a moment the happiness was there. Like the old days. He saw the empty chair. He cleared his throat. He gave his boys a look. The old man managed a smile.

"Guess you should run across the street to your grandma's to have her and your mother walk over for dinner? We've all been through a lot. Seems only right they be here."

Kirk and Jacob said nothing.

WHERE THERE BE DRAGONS

"Pedal faster, Albert," said Emily. "They're catching up."
Her long, golden hair whipped in the wind. She *knew* better than to take Tillman Road. Now that Timmy Whitehead, Oliver Gains, and Conner were chasing them, home seemed a lot farther away.

"I'm going as fast as I can." March winds smacked Albert in the face, slowing his speed. "I'm getting tired."

She didn't like the idea of taking Albert to her hideaway by Egypt Springs, but what choice did she have? One day she saw a cave there. Emily was almost positive no one had uncovered it. Finally, she saw the dirt road ahead, looked back. "Follow me. We'll hide down by the spring."

Albert followed his sister onto a narrow road. Willow trees choked out the sunlight, closing in around them on either side. Loose rock and dirt caused Albert's wheels to lose traction now and then as he took all of it in. Too far to the right would send him off the shoulder for sure. He shuddered at the thought.

They kept riding.

Emily heard the spring. The edge of it was steep with washed out crevices. No place to run. They abandoned their bikes and vanished into the woods.

Emily rolled onto her belly and threw her legs over the edge. She found a rock and lowered herself down. "We don't have to go all the way in," said Emily. "But we might as well."

A spacious lagoon on their right revealed a rock-strewn bottom. Its glassy surface sparkled like gemstones. Large boulders arched around the entrance of the cave and gathered at the foot. Chalky white stones left a fine powder on their hands and clothes as they climbed. The rocks looked a lot like snowballs; perfectly rounded. Albert wondered if a giant might have made them long ago.

At the top they stared down into blackness. Sunlight pooled around the first three feet of space or so before the hand of night gulped it down.

"How do we get down there?" Albert asked. "I don't see a way."

"We'll slide down here and climb out over there." Emily pointed to their left. "See?"

The cave's wall was etched in sunken grooves.

"Want me to go first? I'm your brother, you know."

"No, I'll go first and catch you when you drop."

"But I'm your brother."

"I'm older. Mom and dad'll kill me if something happens to you." She looked at him then. "We don't know what's in there."

"You're right," Albert agreed. "You better go first. You know, see how the land lays."

"Don't follow until I tell you."

"Okay."

Emily sat down and pushed off.

When she hit the ground, clouds of gray dust wafted skyward, choking her. She flailed her arms and rubbed her eyes, then turned her attention to the darkness. She heard dripping water in the distance.

"Emily."

Silence.

He waited.

Nothing.

"You all right?"

Still nothing.

"This isn't funny anymore."

"Gotcha," laughed Emily. "Did I scare you?"

Albert breathed with relief. "No, nine-year-old boys always have heart failure." Giggles drifted up from the cave. "What does it look like?"

"Messy," Emily replied. "It's a cave, silly. You ready?"

Albert slid down the rock face. He saw Emily holding out

her arms to catch him, but was moving too fast to slow his speed. "Look out!" They tumbled backward in a mess of arms and legs. "Thought you were gonna catch me?" Albert stood up. He dusted himself off.

"I would have if you'd slid a little slower, meathead! Hurt?"

"No."

Emily narrowed her eyes. "I can't see anything."

"Spiders and snakes and bats, oh my."

"ALBERT!"

"Sorry."

They moved on.

"You're sure they came this way?" Conner asked. He wasn't feeling brave now. He watched the trees around them. He did not like this. And the look he got from Oliver wasn't brimming with courage either.

"Saw them with my own eyes, guys." Timmy's watchful eyes darted side to side. "Should be right up..."

"I see bikes," said Conner.

"We got them now," Timmy said.

"I don't know about this," Oliver said

"Scared?" Timmy asked.

"No," said Oliver.

"Sure sounds like it to me," added Conner, his own fear yet exposed. "They have to be here somewhere."

"They'll come back for their bikes." Timmy walked to the spring's crest, peered down. "All we have to do is wait."

"Can't wait long," said Conner, climbing from his bike. "I'm late again my dad'll ground me till my hair's gray."

"Excuses. Excuses."

"I second that," said Oliver. "I ain't gettin' grounded cause you want Albert's lunch money."

"What's wrong with you guys? We can't just let him get away. Albert owes me lunch money."

So they waited.

Drags opened his drowsy emerald eyes. The vast seemingly never-ending cave pitter-pattered with thawing ice. His six-foot wings unfolded. He shook off the chill. Finger-thin shafts of sunlight seeped through the dark as he made his way to the mouth of the cave.

Spring had arrived. The dragon slayers had not found him. No slayer ever gambled his life entering a dragon's lair alone. They were sly, but then again, he liked to think himself just as cunning. He was about to continue on, when he heard voices. He stepped back into the gloom from which he came and perked an ear.

"Told you they'd find us," said Albert. "What now?"

"They can't stay out there forever."

"And we can't stay in here, either." Albert stopped. He didn't want to go too deep into the cave. "I should've just paid Timmy."

"Pay?"

"Timmy Whitehead collects lunch money from a few of us. He said if I didn't pay up he'd beat me. I don't like this new town. Nothing's the same. All my friends live in Bender."

Emily knelt down, smiled. "We'll just wait a while. They can't stay out there all day. When we get home we'll tell dad." She didn't like White Ash either. The only good that came with the package was coming to the spring.

"No!" Albert said. "It'll make things worse. I can't have dad fighting my battles."

"Hey, what'd dad tell us a long time ago?"

"Bullies are just as afraid of us as we are of them."

"Right."

"If it's all the same to you, I'd like to stay in here for a while." Albert looked up at his older sister. "Place is kind of nifty."

Drags remained in the shadows, arms across his broad chest, wings folded behind him. The two seemed harmless. What were they wearing? It looked nothing like sheepskins.

Strange.

Bullies. The word left a bitter taste in his mouth. He did not like them. Not one bit. Poor child, he thought. Drags shifted a little too far to the left and knocked a rock off the ledge. It pinged, bounced and lay still on the cave floor. Oh no. The boy and girl stopped.

"What was that?" Emily said.

"Whatever it was it sounded big."

Dust hung in the air as Emily and Albert crept deeper into the cave. The dark swallowed them.

"How far back does it go?" asked Albert.

"Have no idea. Stay close and be careful."

"I'm scared, Emily."

"Nothing to be afraid of." she soothed him. "Here," she took his hand. "Better?"

"Much."

Something large and looming shifted in the dark.

"Far enough," said Emily. "Let's go back."

They backed away from the dark. The form closed the gap.

"Please don't go," Drags spoke softly. He remained unseen.

Emily backed away. Albert's grip was so tight she thought she might lose her hand. "Please don't hurt us. We're leaving."

"This is my home," his voice boomed. "Who might you be?"

It's a crazy person. I knew this was a bad idea, thought Emily. "We're sorry," Emily said, backing away. "We didn't mean to…"

Albert's grip loosened. "What's your name?"

"Drags."

He pulled his hand away from his sister.

"Albert!"

"I'll not harm the child, lass," said Drags.

"We can't see you," said Albert. "Can you come out?"

"I'm afraid my…" His words trailed off. "I don't want to scare you."

"You've done that," Emily said.

A chuckle in the dark bloomed. "Yes, I suppose I have." The voice moved as it talked. "Here," the voice said. "I'll come out into the light, but please don't be afraid. I wish you no harm."

Drags' massive head practically took up the entire entryway; three misshapen horns protruded from his head. His tail, thin and powerful, moved to and fro.

Albert managed a squeal of delight. "A dragon!" He could barely contain himself.

Emily never believed in dragons. She didn't believe in anything she couldn't touch, smell, or feel.

The dragon's lips peeled away, revealing a row of razor sharp teeth. "I'm amazed by your words." He stretched. "May I join this adventure?"

Albert leaped up and down, clapping. "This is gonna be great! Let Timmy Whitehead pick on me now."

"Albert, please." Even though she was afraid, Emily tried desperately to keep it hidden.

"You're not going to eat us, are you?" Emily asked.

"Good heavens, child," Drags said. "What kind of dragon do you think I am? If I tried, you'd run back to your village, tell the king, and then the dragon slayers would come for me."

Albert tugged at Emily's coat sleeve. "King? dragon slayers? Has he lost his mind?"

"Drags, there is no king," said Emily. "And dragon slayers are only in books."

"Every land has a king, lass," Drags pointed out. "Here, I'll prove it." He moved past them, applied weight behind one of the boulders and pushed. The boulder tumbled away with little effort and splashed into the lagoon. A wave of light and gust of chilly wind bathed all three of them.

"You see that!" Conner leaped back.

"Quit being a chicken, Conner. Just fell is all," Timmy said.

"Looked like it was pushed." Oliver swallowed. "I think..."

"We better go down there and see what's what," Timmy completed Oliver's sentence with a sneer. "Got a problem with that?"

Oliver grimaced, looked at Conner for backup. There was none. He shrugged. "Only if we're going down there." Running now would only get him thumped. Oliver knew that Timmy had no problems working him over.

"And we are, so I guess we have a problem." Timmy faced forward.

"Gonna thump me?"

"Thinking about it," said Timmy as he removed his jacket.

"Enough," Conner jumped in. "Timmy and I will go down. You stay up here and keep a look out." He didn't like the idea, but he didn't want Oliver getting thumped either. Conner has known Timmy longer and pretty much gets away with murder. However, the look in Timmy's eyes was anything but pleasing.

"Sounds like a plan to me," said Oliver, glanced at Conner with a wink, and mouthed the word *thanks*.

Timmy and Conner climbed down the ledge.

"This can't be right," Drags said. "Everything has changed. What has happened here? Everything's gone."

What was once green pastures and towering evergreens and wheat fields somehow, someway, turned into a land unlike what he remembered. "The village," Drags was near fright. "The village is—"

"Drags, it's all right."

"No, it's not all right." Drags stepped away from the entrance. "The village is gone! The…goodness me. What's happened?"

"Drags," Albert said, running up to the frightened dragon. "We'll be your friends."

"That's very kind, but my eyes deceive me. This can't be! How on earth will I hunt? The king has proven to be a great adversary and slayer in his own right and will launch an attack if I'm seen. This is not good. I wish Drago were here. He'd know what to do."

"Drago?" Albert looked up into the dragon's eyes.

"My elder brother. He was once the most feared and hunted dragon in all the land. The king offered eighty gold coins to any slayer who fought the mighty dragon and won." Drags shuffled the two children deeper into the cave. "We must be careful. For a human to be seen with the likes of me is considered an act of defiance against the king."

"Drags," Emily looked up into the soft-wrinkled eyes of their new friend. "There is no king."

"She's telling the truth," added Albert. "Drago? Is he here, too?"

"Lad," Drags spoke ever so softly, "I'm afraid he won't be joining us this day." He fell silent, and then, "He has passed on to the other side."

"The other side?"

"Where all dragons go when their time here is finished. It's a place of many magnificent colors, rivers, dark lush grasslands, and towering trees."

"What was he like?" Emily asked, found a rock and sat down.

"Drago?"

"Of course," Albert said. "We'd love to hear. Did he fight the dragon slayers?"

Drags laughter poured out. "And much more, he was. Why, in the old days, Kings paid great sums of gold and silver for a dragon's head. But like I said, Drago was feared; not by just the king and the slayers, but by all." Drags rubbed his hands together, licked his chops. "Sorry, just excited to tell the story, is all.

"I was only a draglit when the first of many slayers came to lay claim to the mighty Drago. We watched him fight from afar as he battled the armor-plated men, and Drago triumphed. That made King Richard furious, so he sent his most prized slayers, and they too were defeated. Imagine fighting hundreds of men, lad." He stared at Albert. "Drago stood a hundred feet tall with wings as wide and as long as a clipper ship, I'll tell you."

"What finally beat him?" Emily coaxed.

Drags muzzle seemed to wilt. His eyes hardened. "Well, it was spring, and the slayers, like most smart knights, never enter a dragon's lair, you see, but they did wait for him to wake. A dragon is most weak the first few days they open their eyes, just as I am now." He yawned, and when he exhaled a bright ball of fire shot out of his mouth. "Goodness me," chuckled Drags. "My mother always told me never to shoot fireballs in the cave." He shrugged playfully. "Once a draglit always a draglit, right?"

Albert and Emily laughed.

"Anyway, the slayers waited for him to step out of the cave and then attacked. Drago never had a chance. They said it was fast and painless." Drags went silent for a while, and then, "Seems you have trouble of your own."

"Trouble?" Emily said.

"Have you not bullies outside waiting for you?"

"I almost forgot, thanks Drags," said Albert. "We figured we'd stay in here in hopes they'd go away."

"You don't mind do you, Drags?" Emily shot him a look.

"Not at all, but don't you think you should confront this threat?" Drags placed a massive clawed hand on their shoulders. "You know, your father speaks with great truth. They're just as afraid of you."

"Easier said than done, my friend. Three of them and two of us."

"Correction," said the dragon. "Three against three sounds to me like even odds."

Albert leaped off the rock, danced about the cave like a prizefighter, punching air.

"Not what I had in mind, little man." Drags moved passed them, heading toward the cave's opening.

"What're you doing?" Emily stood.

"A dragon's sense of territory can be most helpful."

"What's that mean?" asked Albert.

"It means they're coming."

"Oh no," Emily shuffled after Drags, as Albert followed.

"You're going to eat them, aren't you?"

"My dear boy," said Drags, "what's with you and eating people? I'm not that kind of dragon."

Drags glanced at Emily. "He always like this?"

"Afraid so."

"How do you eat then?"

"Good heavens, with my mouth, child."

"Then you do eat people."

"He won't stop," Emily reassured him.

"What do I eat?"

"Yes."

"Little boys that talk too much."

Albert instantly went silent.

The dragon roared with laughter.

Finally at the bottom, Timmy looked up at Oliver, gave a thumbs up, turned and watchfully made his way with Conner toward the cave. Conner followed close, his arms outstretched for balance, watching Timmy slip a time or two. The rocks just beneath the water's shore was slick with moss.

Steadying himself, Conner took his eyes off Timmy and searched the water, half expecting something to tear through the glassy surface and gobble them up, but that didn't happen. Too bad it's too cold for a swim, he thought, and returned to the mission.

At the cave Timmy stopped, looked back. "Climb up and tell me what you see."

"Me?"

"Yes, you," Timmy said. "I've got your back."

Not keen on climbing boulders, much less going inside the cave, Conner felt his face heat up. "This was your idea, not mine."

"Scared?"

"Just as much as you are."

"Am not," scoffed Timmy.

For the first time ever, Conner saw the color drain from Timmy's face. He was afraid. That much was fact. "Monday morning while you're pushing kids around, I'll spill my guts about you being afraid of some stupid little cave; that I was the first one in and you wouldn't go."

"Better not!"

"And I'm sure Oliver will back the story." Conner noticed Timmy's face soften. He had him.

Unwilling, Timmy climbed the first boulder and vanished into the cave.

Conner followed.

The cave bottom was powdery and the walls glistened with moisture. When Conner arrived at Timmy's side they moved onward.

"See anything?" Conner didn't want to make any more noise than needed.

"Not yet."

Ahead was a bend in the cave.

It was dark.

"I don't like this, Conner."

"Too late, tough guy. We aren't turning back now," Conner said. "Remember what I told you outside. Don't think I won't tell."

"I remember," I'll fix his goose later, Timmy thought, if there is a later.

In front of them a cloud of dust kicked up and out came the biggest leg Timmy and Conner had ever seen. The second leg joined the first. Drags stared down sternly, his mouth opened wide, arms outstretched as his pointed tongue slithered. "BE YOU DRAGON SLAYERS!"

The cave shook with such force that Timmy and Conner fell over themselves screaming, but before they could make their escape, Drags whipped out his arms and snatched up the two by their collars. "I smell dragon slayers in my lair!" his voice boomed. "Eat you up, eat you up."

"No, please!" Timmy struggled in the dragon's grasp, as did Conner. "We didn't..."

"Silence!"

"He made me come in," Conner said

"I said silence!" roared the voice. "Only one can save you now, my little slayers." Drags' voice shook the bats awake. The cave suddenly alive with them, he breathed fire over the boys' heads. "Leave this place and never return and tell no one what you've seen. If ever you bother my friends Emily or Albert..." He thought a moment, and then, "or any other child, I'll hunt you down. Never will you bully another soul!"

"We promise!"

"Yeah, we'll stop!" Conner added.

"Then be gone with you." Drags lowered them and watched them tear out of the cave.

Drags barely contained his laughter as Emily and Albert danced around the cave.

And then it happened.

The dragon watched as Timmy slipped off the rocks. A splash followed.

"Oh, my!" Drags raced forward with lightning speed, Albert and Emily following. He looked out. The boy was sinking fast. He reached out with a mighty arm, plunged his hand into the icy waters, and pulled the boy to safety. He gently placed him inside the cave, glimpsed around for the other boy. Drags found him on the shore with his face buried in his hands weeping.

"You need not cry, child," Drags spoke softly.

Conner looked up. He mopped tears away from his eyes. "He fell in the water, though."

"He's fine," said Drags. "Come see."

Timmy trembled from the cold. He wiped tears away with the back of his hand. Drags breathed ever so gently on the boy, drying him.

"That better?" asked the dragon.

Timmy nodded, smiled up at the dragon. "Thanks."

"Will he be okay?" Conner climbed down into the cave. He watched the dragon closely.

"He'll be fine," Drags said. He looked back to Timmy. "It is I who should be sorry, little man." He tried to smile, but found it very hard. "It was very mean of me to scare you like that. I think we all have learnt a priceless lesson today." Timmy could not take his eyes off the dragon. "It takes a bigger man to be a leader than one that follows, Timmy. Wouldn't you rather lead and teach than to cause hurt feelings?"

Albert walked out from behind Drags. "I'm sorry you fell in the lagoon, Timmy."

Timmy got up and brushed himself off. "And I'm sorry for taking your lunch money, too, Albert. In fact, I don't feel good about any of it. Not at all." His hands were in his pockets. He kicked dirt with his shoes. For the first time in his life, he was ashamed.

Conner was picking his fingernails. His face was red with guilt as well. "Yeah, we're sorry, Albert."

They all shook hands.

It was a good day, thought Drags.

A shout came from the cave's mouth. "You find them yet? Need help?" Oliver asked, climbing the rocks. "I'm coming in!" He froze when he landed on his feet. "Jumpin' bullfrogs, guys!" Eyes wide, mouth open, Oliver felt a scream coming but it refused to exit his mouth as if it were afraid to.

"Calm down, Oliver," Timmy said. He looked up at Drags. "This is our friend, Oliver. Oliver, this is Drags." He introduced them.

The dragon bowed.

"Is this for real?"

"As real as it gets," replied Conner. "Cool, huh?"

Emily had not said a word as the hair on the nape of her neck suddenly stiffened, her insides going cold. She sensed something else was inside the cave with them. Her spine stiffened, goose bumps tickled her as she turned slowly.

Drags and Albert, unaware of this new threat, cheered, leaped, and laughed heartedly about making new friends when an unexpected tremor shook the entire cave. Along the walls, torches came to life, giving the circular room light.

The cheers died away as fear slipped into the group's circle. A hulking figure framed the east wall, a beast much broader and taller than Drags.

It moved toward them. "Son?"

"Father?" Drags moved to his father's side and looked up into aging eyes. "We were just...I thought..."

"That place is forbidden, my son."

"It is not our world?"

"No. It leads to a world not like our own. Dangerous places thrive on the other side more savage than our own."

"I didn't know, father."

All of the kids were stunned by this new discovery.

Drags' father gave them the once over. "And who might this be?"

"They're my friends. They live on the other side." An idea sparked. "Can they come with us?"

"Same thing as with us, son. They cannot cross into our world either. It is unsafe. King Richard has a new army and swears by his knighthood each and every dragon will fall by his sword, and there is always the pending threat of the Dreadlocks."

"What are Dreadlocks?" Emily was unafraid now, curious.

"Dreadlocks dwell in the east. A place we call *Badlands*. Hideous creatures that roam the land. Merely parasites to our clans."

"Allow them a glimpse of our world, father. I have witnessed a portion of theirs, after all."

His father was silent and said, "Very well. But I must insist you speak of nothing you see."

They followed the tunnel lit by torches. A light momentarily blinded the five children as they neared an opening in the cave.

What they saw next reminded them of fairy tales; sloping hills and gorges, green pastures, oceans of trees on all sides of a large lake. The sky blue water reflected a radiant sun. Dragons drank from the shore while others flew overhead like wild birds.

"Do you like?" Drags moved beyond them, inhaled a lung full of air, and wheeled his head at a ninety-degree angle. "This is my home."

"Oh yes," said Emily. She didn't want to ever leave.

"This is so not happening," Timmy smiled with glee.

Albert ambled out from beneath the cave's overhanging lip and giggled with excitement. "Can we come back in the spring time, Drags?"

"That would be wonderful!" added Emily.

"I'm in," Conner said.

"Same here," added Oliver.

Timmy walked out and stood beside Albert. "It's magical, isn't it?"

"Indeed it is," Drags' attention fell to his father.

"Very well, but only in the spring, and not out in the open. And now that you have seen our world, it is time to go. Drags, please return them to their world."

Drags did as he was told and took them back to the entrance of the cave.

"And we'll see you next spring, right?" Albert grew very sad. "Promise we'll do things next time."

"Albert!" Emily tugged at his coat sleeve.

"I promise." Drags patted his new friends and said his goodbyes as all five left the cave.

The dragon kept his word and allowed the kids back to the cave time and again. Albert taught Timmy how to swim, while Emily read stories to them all. It was a time when dreams were made among monsters and children.

As time passed, Drags watched all of them grow. He said his farewell to Timmy, Conner, and Oliver as they left for a place called college. He was proud of them, proud because they became leaders of their own lives.

They never returned to White Ash.

A pact was then sealed between Drags, Albert and Emily for seasons, years, and decades. One day Albert and Emily grew too old to climb down to the cave, so Drags went to them. They wanted to run through the cave and play as children. To swim in the lagoon, but time had caught up with them.

Many years following that sunlit day, Emily appeared on the shore alone. Drags went to her. Their friendship rooted, the dragon hugged her tight. They shared passing moments through the year; mourned Albert's passing; and when they parted, he watched her return to her metal carriage and drive away. He waved with tears in his eyes.

The following spring, Drags waited by the boulders all day for Emily. He watched the sun come up and go down three times, and still no Emily. The same thing happened the next year and the year after that.

He never saw her again.

Some say if you drive out to Egypt Springs on a warm summer evening you can catch an ember of light inside a cave and a dragon longing to see his friends again.

ABOUT THE AUTHOR

Steven Lloyd writes out of Southern Illinois, and has interviewed such authors and actors as Jack Ketchum, Nancy Collins, legendary film greats Bill Moseley and Sid Haig, from the "Devil's Rejects" films. His work has appeared in several print and online publications.

In 2008 Lloyd launched a publishing company called Croatoan Publishing, dedicated to the Horror and Dark Suspense genre. Before closing the doors, he released People are Strange by James Newman and Flesh Welder by Ronald Kelly.

Visit him on the Webat:

http://stevenlloyd.weebly.com/index.html

Curious about other Crossroad Press books?
Stop by our site:
http://store.crossroadpress.com
We offer quality writing
in digital, audio, and print formats.

Enter the code FIRSTBOOK
to get 20% off your first order from our store!
Stop by today!

28739114R00066

Made in the USA
Lexington, KY
25 January 2019